DIAMONDS IN THE DUST
DIAMONDS ARE FOREVER TRILOGY (BOOK 1)

CHARMAINE PAULS

Published by Charmaine Pauls

Montpellier, 34090, France

www.charmainepauls.com

Published in France

This is a work of fiction. Names, characters, and incidents depicted in this book are products of the author's imagination or are used fictitiously. Any resemblance to actual events, locales, organizations, or persons, living or dead, is entirely coincidental and beyond the intent of the author or the publisher. No part of this book may be reproduced in any form or by any electronic or mechanical means, including photocopying, recording, information storage and retrieval systems, without written permission from the author, except for the use of brief quotations in a book review.

Copyright © 2020 by Charmaine Pauls

All rights reserved.

Photography by Wander Aguiar Photography LLC

Cover model Rodiney Santiago

Cover design by Okay Creations

ISBN: 978-2-491833-01-5 (eBook)

ISBN: 979-8-565851-60-1 (Print)

❦ Created with Vellum

PROLOGUE

The screaming in the kitchen turns louder. Mommy and Daddy's voices travel through the thin wall and sting my ears. It doesn't hurt like when I had an ear infection, but it hurts in my chest, and I'm really scared.

I crouch in the corner on the bed I share with my brother, Damian, and hold Vanessa, my doll, close. I wish Damian was here, but it's Sunday, and he's delivering newspapers.

A thump shakes the bunker beds of my older brothers, Leon and Ian, against the opposite wall. Cups and plates rattle on the other side.

"Always the fucking same." Daddy's voice is too loud.

The neighbors will hear. I cringe, because they'll look at me weird tomorrow when I play on the stairs.

"You're all the fucking same."

My heart flaps like the wings of that poor bird I saw in the awful cage in Auntie May's kitchen with the poo scattered around it on the floor. I concentrate on the moldy patches on the wall and the crack that runs down the middle, holding my breath as I wait for the next thud to shake the floor. The dark stain in the corner looks like the head of a wolf with a long snout and a floppy ear. The one in the middle looks like a flower growing from the crack.

I knew it was coming, but when something crashes against the other side of the wall, I gasp quietly, careful not to make noise.

"It's all right," I whisper to Vanessa, clutching her tighter. I wish my name was something pretty like Vanessa. I hate my name. Zoe is a stupid name.

"How many times must I tell you, woman?" Daddy bellows. "You don't—"

Mommy's voice is shrill. "You don't tell me what to do!"

I lay Vanessa on the bed, trembling as I try to block out the angry voices. "Shh." She stares at me with big, happy eyes, but I know she's just as scared as I am. I know how to smile to look brave.

Maybe they'll stop.

Sometimes, they do.

I push Vanessa's arm through the hole I've cut from one of granny's napkins with Mommy's nail scissors and tie the ends in a knot. It doesn't matter that she only has one arm. It's a pretty dress all the same.

Something crashes. The noise is sharp and dull, like when grandpa chops wood.

"I'll fucking kill us all!" Daddy shouts.

Mommy's footsteps fall hard on the floor. "Don't touch me! I'll stab you! I'm not kidding, you fucking prick!"

It hurts to breathe. My eyes burn and tears start to drip. They plop on my hands, warm and wet. I'm dizzy and hot, like when I had the flu. Scrambling off the bed, I grab Vanessa and my book and dash down the short hallway to the broom closet at the end.

Please don't let them see me.

I close my eyes as I pass the kitchen door, but nobody calls my name or grabs the collar of my dress. The closet door squeaks as I open it and slip inside the darkness that smells of shoe polish and dust. I close it tightly, so tightly you can't even see the light through the crack, and feel under the cushions on the scratchy blanket of my nest for the flashlight. Huddling in the corner of my hiding place, I flick on the light and rock with Vanessa and my book in my arms.

The book is big and heavy. It's my only other possession, and I take it everywhere I go. The pages are dirty from all the times I've licked my fingers to separate them. Damian says they have dog ears, although I'm not sure where he sees the dogs. When I ask him, he just laughs at me. The spine is cracked and slack with stitches sticking out like my dresses when Mommy takes out the seams so I can wear them another year. When I open the book, it falls open at the same place it always does, on the first page of my favorite story about the princess and the frog.

The tinkling of breaking glass pierces my safe place. Pinching my eyes shut, I block out the terrible sound that's scarier than monsters.

More stuff falls over somewhere.

I force myself to open my eyes and look at the picture. I know each outline and every color of the princess in her puffy, pink dress, the golden ball lying next to the pond, the green leaves of the water lilies, and the frog sitting on them.

Pushing my finger on the page, I drag it along the letters as I whisper, "Once upon a time..."

I can't read yet, but I know the story by heart.

"...there was a beautiful princess who lived in a castle."

The book is like magic. The world in the story becomes real, and the sounds coming from down the hallway fade as I turn into the princess in the pink dress, standing next to the pond on the softest, greenest grass in my silk slippers with my golden ball. I'm a beautiful girl with yellow hair just like in the picture, not the boring color of dark-brown coffee like my own hair, and—

I jerk when the door opens.

"Hey, Zee," Damian says, calling me by his special name for me when his face appears in the crack. "Can I come in?"

He doesn't wait for me to say yes. He crawls in, bending double to fit under the shelf because he's ten and not only twice my age, but also twice my size.

When he's closed the door and settled opposite me, he asks, "What are you reading?"

The space is so small even with our knees pulled up our legs press together.

Sniffing, I shrug. He knows the stories by heart, too, because he's the one reading them to me. It's not like I have another book.

He nudges me. "Want me to read it to you?"

I shrug again but turn the book around for him to see the letters.

He ruffles my hair. "Next year, when you go to school, you'll learn to read, then you don't have to wait for me, and you can read other books, better books."

I hold Vanessa tighter. "I like it when you read to me. I like *these* stories."

Ian and Leon are older. When they're not in school, they're in the street with their friends, getting up to no good as Mommy always says. I don't see them much, and when I do, they mostly tease me. Damian is only in grade five and not allowed to go out in the street alone after school. He has to stay and look after me, so Mommy won't be cross when she comes home from work.

"You won't want to read these silly stories anymore when you're in school," he says.

Fresh tears prick behind my eyes. "They're not silly."

"This isn't like life at all," he says, sounding all grownup.

I jut out my chin. "It is, too."

"Is not."

"Is, too! One day, I'll find a prince, and marry him, and be a princess, and live in a castle, and we'll live happily ever after. You'll see."

His sigh is deep and heavy, sounding just like Daddy when he comes back from a day of what he calls *deep diggin'*. I always imagine *deep mine diggin'* to be making a big hole in the middle of a lawn for a sparkling blue swimming pool.

"Life isn't a fairytale, Zee. There's no knight on a white horse who's going to rescue you. You have to do it yourself."

Pressing my hands over my ears, I block him out. I block out the nasty words, because they're not true. I know they're not.

He pulls away my hands. "I'm not telling you this to be mean. I'm telling you this, so you won't be disappointed one day."

"Stop it," Mommy yells.

A glass shatters somewhere.

"You want me to stop, huh?" Daddy yells back. "Why not destroy everything?"

"You know what?" Mommy is sobbing. "Go ahead. Break everything. That's all you're good for, you son of a lousy bitch."

A curse. A loud bang. Then, the awful, awful silence.

Sometimes, the silence is worse. Daddy won't come home until tomorrow. Mommy will cry all night and not come out of her room. Damian will butter toast, and we'll eat it under the tent he'll make of our blanket on our bed, but there's nowhere to hide from the guilt.

Father Mornay says guilt is good because it tells us when we've done something wrong. I don't like feeling guilty. Mommy will scream at us and say it's our fault, all because there are so many mouths to feed. I'll feel really bad and not know how to be better or less of a mouth to feed.

Daddy will come home stumbling up the stairs and crashing into furniture, and he'll ignore Mommy and be angry with us. He'll give me a hiding for not cleaning the kitchen, even if the dishes are done. He'll take his belt to Damian for not taking out the trash, even if the trashcan is empty. I'll cry quietly in our room, and Damian will get broody and glary-eyed, but Daddy won't touch Ian or Leon. They're too big, almost as tall as Daddy, and stronger.

"Once upon a time…" Damian starts, his voice cracking a little as if it's on the brink of breaking, becoming deeper like Ian's, "…there was a princess…"

One day, Damian will be strong and tall, too.

I don't care what Damian says. One day, I'll find my prince. He'll buy me beautiful dresses and lots of pretty glasses, and he'll never break them. He'll take me very, very far away from here, and I'll never come back. Just wait and see.

CHAPTER 1

Johannesburg, South Africa

Zoe

My gaze is trained on the pavement to keep from stepping in the dog poo that litters the four blocks from the sweatshop to my apartment, but I'm not present in the glorious summer afternoon. My thoughts are where they usually dwell, dreaming up fantastic plans of escaping the hellhole I'm living in. Dreaming makes my existence more bearable. Dreaming *is* my escape.

Near the flea market, the air is thick and heavy with the smell of carbon from the coal train tracks. Everything underneath the train bridge is gray, covered in layers of soot and smog. I glance at the sky. Up there, the air is blue and clear, pure and unobtainable.

With a sigh, I fall in line at the fresh produce stall, using the waiting time to stretch my sore muscles. My back aches from being bent over a sewing machine all day. In my head, I count how far the coins I have left in my purse will go. The end of the month is always the worst, but on the upside, payday is around the corner. When it's my turn, I take a banana and two tomatoes.

I drag myself the last two blocks home, weary to the bone. I'm eager to feed my empty stomach and soak in a warm bath. Then I'll collapse into bed with my new stack of library books.

At my building, I curse under my breath. The door that gives access to the street is ajar. The lock is broken again, and it will take ages before it's fixed. The landlord doesn't maintain the building. That's why the façade is black with years' worth of grime and the inside walls moldy from permanent damp.

With my gaze trained on the floor so I don't step on one of the cats always begging for food, I push the door open with a shoulder while balancing my tote in one hand and my shopping bag in the other. The gloomy entrance is quiet, strangely absent from meows and furry bodies rubbing against my legs.

My eyes are still adjusting from the bright daylight to the somber interior. The light switch has been broken for years. I frown, scouting the stairs in the sliver of light that falls in from outside before the door swings shut with a creak and basks the space in semi-darkness. The weak glow from the single bulb on the upstairs landing is the only light preventing the inhabitants from not tripping on the stairs.

I'm about to call for the cats when something crashes into me from behind. My mouth opens on a scream, but no sound escapes as a large hand clamps over my mouth and an arm knocks the wind from my stomach as it wraps around my waist and lifts me off my feet.

The bags in my hands drop to the floor. Fear slams into my chest. In a distant corner of my mind, I notice the tomatoes that roll to the foot of the stairs, and a logical, detached part of me worries about the spoiled food even as I start fighting for my life. I twist and buck. With my arms constrained at my sides, I can only kick. I try to bite, but I can't force my lips apart. The hold over my mouth is too tight. It feels as if my jaw is about to snap. A button on my blouse pops from my efforts. It drops on the floor with a clink and bounces three, four, five times before it finally surrenders quietly in some corner. A smell of spices and citrus invades my nostrils—a man's cologne. My senses are heightened. In the life that passes in front of my eyes, everything seems louder and clearer.

"Shh," a male voice says against my ear, only making my terror spike.

I want to twist my head to the side to evaluate the threat, but I can't turn my neck. Two men manifest from the shadows. One has long, blond hair and the other is bald with a beard. They move quickly. The blond one snatches up my bags while the bearded one goes up the stairs. He looks left and right before giving a nod.

At the signal, my captor follows with me. I have to breathe through my nose as he climbs the single flight of stairs to my floor. Like this, the smell of the urine on the stairs and the mold on the walls is stronger. It makes me gag. Or maybe it's how our bodies are pressed together, and what he has in store for me.

The blond has taken my keys from my bag and has the door to my apartment open by the time we hit the landing. I glance at my neighbor's door, praying to God Bruce isn't playing his X-Box with his headphones on, but the sounds of his favorite game hits me before the stranger carries me inside.

Lowering me to the floor, he keeps his hand over my mouth. "My men are going to leave." His voice is deep and his accent strong. The way he rolls the R makes the dangerous words sound sensual. "I don't want to hurt you, Zoe, but if you scream, I'll have to. Understand?"

Dear God. He knows my name. I pinch my eyes shut, my chest heaving with every breath. How does he know my name?

He speaks softly, pressing the words to my ear. "I asked you a question."

I give a tight nod. What choice do I have?

He removes his hand slowly. "That's better."

The minute he releases me, I spin around and back up to the couch. "I don't have money. I have nothing valuable."

He smiles. "Do I look like I need to steal money?"

I take him in. His face is square with sharp lines, his nose slightly askew as if it has been broken many times. Thick, black hair is styled with fashionable sideburns. The tone of his skin is warm, but his eyes are cold, their color the gray of an overcast sky. He's not a handsome man, and the broken skin of his knuckles tells its own story.

Swallowing, I drop my gaze to his body. He's taller and broader than anyone I've seen. His chest and legs fill out every inch of his suit. It's a gray pinstripe—pure wool, judging by the thread—but it's the perfect cut that differentiates him. He screams money and power. No, he wouldn't have broken in for money. The alternative makes me break out in a cold sweat.

He advances on me, his gaze slipping to my chest. "However, you do have something of value I need."

I look down. My blouse is flaring where the button tore off, exposing my bra. Clutching the ends together, I ask through trembling lips, "What?"

When he nods at the two men, I look over at them. The blond one has a model-pretty face. He's lean and tall. The one with the beard is stockier with eyes so black the pupils bleed into the irises. Both are dressed in dark suits and carry guns.

The bearded man goes through my tote, unpacking the overall I use for work on the table with my purse and hairbrush. The bag with my banana lies next to it. He picked up my tomatoes, the split skins visible through the transparent plastic. When he finds my phone, he hands it to the man who grabbed me. The man pockets it. Then, like my captor promised, his men leave. The key sounds in the lock. I'm locked in with the stranger.

Fear heats me from the inside, making me feel nauseous. Even my hunger disappears. "What do you want from me?"

The man doesn't answer. As soon as his accomplices are gone, he turns his attention from me to inspecting my living space. His gaze moves from the ratty couch with the broken springs to the framed photos on the wall and finally to the daisy in the vase on the table. His evaluation is invasive. I know what he sees, but I refuse to be ashamed of my poverty, especially in front of a man with an expensive suit who snatched me off the street.

He walks to the daisy and touches the stem. "Nice touch."

"What?"

"The flower." Meticulously, he strokes every petal. "Where did you get it?"

What the heck does that matter? "From the pavement."

He gives me a doubtful smile. "You didn't take it from someone's garden."

Despite my fear, my anger blooms. "No, I didn't *steal* it. It grows wild."

He doesn't react to the silent accusation. He only continues to watch me intently. After a moment, he asks, "A boyfriend didn't give it to you?"

"No." Where is he going with his line of questioning? Why doesn't he tell me what he wants?

"No boyfriend, then."

"No." I watch him as he moves to the wall to study the photos, my heart pounding like a pendulum against my ribs.

"Your family?"

"Yes."

He points at the tallest boy on the yellowed Polaroid picture. "Who's this?"

"Why do you care?"

He looks back at me with a quiet warning in his eyes. He doesn't need his foreign-sounding words to instill fear.

"That's Ian," I say reluctantly, "my oldest brother."

"The others?"

"Next to him is Leon, then Damian, and me."

Leaning closer, he studies the girl with the pigtails and too short dress. "You were cute. How old were you?"

I grip my blouse tighter. "Ten."

He motions at Mom and Dad. "These are your parents?"

"Late parents."

"My condolences."

He picks up the book about Venice from the couch and turns the cover. I don't want him to touch it. I don't want this man who stole into my privacy to also invade my dreams. My dreams are mine. They're private, but I'm helpless from stopping him as his gaze skims over the table of contents and the library stamp before he drops it back onto the couch and opens the book on the coffee table. It's on loan from the library, too, about the same topic, just like the book next to the bath and the one on my nightstand. When he's done inspecting that one, he goes to the bookshelf and tilts his head to read the titles. Shelf by shelf, he goes through them.

Losing interest in the books, he makes his way to the kitchen. He stops in the doorframe and assesses the shelf with two chipped glasses and a dented pot, the only inherited items that haven't yet broken or rusted. His attention moves to the geranium on the windowsill. The sturdy, green plant is my pride and hope. I found it in the trash and managed to save it. Whoever discarded it must've thought it was dead, but there was still a tiny bit of green in the stalk. It was dry, neglected, and I felt sorry for it. The fact that it fought and survived to bloom and thrive is a reminder to myself to never to give up.

He looks at the darker square on the lanoline floor where the fridge used to stand. I long since sold it when I couldn't pay the rent, just like the rest of the furniture and everything else that were worth a few bucks. Without groceries, I don't need a fridge. A few minutes ago, where tomorrow's dinner was going to come from was my biggest problem. I never imagined my life could get worse.

Suddenly tired, I hug myself. "Look, just tell me why you're here and then leave me alone."

He doesn't acknowledge me. He's staring at the food cupboard. Instead of a door, it's covered with a curtain, which I left open, exposing the almost empty jar of peanut butter and crust of bread.

"I suppose an introduction is in order," he says when he finally turns back to me. "Since I already know your name, it seems only fair."

"I don't want to know your name," I blurt out. The less I know, the better my chances of survival.

He extends a hand. "Maxime Belshaw."

My shaking gets worse. This doesn't look good for me. When I don't move, he strides over, grips my fingers, and presses his lips to my knuckles. The gesture seems taunting instead of chivalrous, and I yank my hand away from his touch.

"Now that we know each other, *Zo*, we're going to have a conversation."

"Don't call me that." Only people who care about me call me Zo.

He raises a brow. "Isn't that what your friends call you?"

The fact that he knows is disturbing. "Exactly. They're *friends*."

Rather than upset, he appears amused. "Zoe, then. Your older brothers, they left town a long time ago. Am I right?"

"If this is about Ian or Leon, I haven't heard from them since they left."

"No." Reaching out slowly, he drags a thumb along my jaw. "This isn't about them."

The gentleness of the touch catches me off guard. I have to bend backward to escape the odd caress because my calves are pressed against the couch.

"This is about Damian," he says.

When he drops his hand, I straighten, trying to hold his gaze without letting him see the fear in my eyes.

"This is how our talk is going to work," he says. "I'm going to ask you a few questions, and you're going to answer them."

"Never."

I'm not ratting on Damian. Of all the people in our dysfunctional family, he's the only one who cares. Damian is only five years older than me, but he single-handedly raised me. He looked out for me when no one else did. He's suffered enough. He didn't deserve any of the terrible things that have happened to him.

Maxime looks me over. "You're tougher than I expected. The poor ones usually break easily."

My anger makes me forget to be frightened. "Fuck you."

"Did I hit a nerve?"

"Go to hell," I hiss.

"Fine. We'll play it your way." He takes his phone from his pocket and swipes over the screen.

My heart pumps so furiously I feel every beat in my temples. He rests the phone against the book on the coffee table with the screen turned toward me. A video call connects. The video and audio functions on his side are deactivated. Whoever he's connecting to can't see or hear us.

A second later, an image fills the screen. I freeze. A chill runs down my spine. Maxime's cronies are next door with Bruce, and my neighbor is tied up in a chair.

"Bruce!" I jump for the phone, but Maxime easily grabs me, holding me by my arms. I struggle in his hold, but I'm no match for his strength. "What are you doing to him?"

"Quiet," Maxime says.

I try to kick him, but he easily restrains me.

"Why are you doing this?" I cry out, fighting to free myself while his fingers dig harder into my flesh.

The bald bastard pulls back his arm and plants his fist in Bruce's face. The chair topples over, Bruce landing on his back.

"No!" I strain forward, trying to reach the phone, but Maxime holds me tightly.

The guard picks up the chair. Bruce spits blood, his eyes filled with venom as he glares at his assailant. The bastard hits him again, this time with a blow on the jaw that sends his face flying sideways.

"Stop it," I scream. "Leave him alone."

Bruce grunts as fists fall on his stomach and ribs. A vicious blow splits his eyebrow open. I can't watch any more. My legs buckle. Sobbing, I fall to my knees. Maxime's grip moves to my hair. His fingers fasten in the bun I always wear to work. Pulling my head back, he forces me to meet his eyes.

"Are you ready to have a conversation now?"

"Please, stop," I say through my tears. "I'll tell you what you want to know."

He picks up the phone, flicks a finger over the screen, and says, "Give it a break."

After pocketing the phone, he takes my elbows to help me to my feet. Gently almost, he wipes the tears from my cheeks. "It doesn't have to be like this. It can be as easy or difficult as you make it." He pushes me down onto the couch.

Teeth chattering, I scoot into the corner, getting as far away from him as I can.

"Stay there," he says.

He goes to the kitchen. The pipes creak as he opens the tap. A moment later, he returns with a glass of water, which he pushes into my hand.

"Drink," he says.

I take a sip on autopilot, even if I'm not thirsty.

He sits down so close to me our bodies touch. "Let's have that little chat. Are you and Damian close?"

I nod, unable to stop the tears running down my cheeks.

"Shh." He threads his fingers through my hair, massaging my scalp. A pin comes loose and drops into my lap. "Do you visit him in jail?"

I shake my head.

"Use your voice, Zoe."

The word comes out on a croak. "No."

"Good. You're doing well." He twists a lock of hair that came free from my bun around his finger. "Why not?"

"He doesn't want me to visit."

"Why's that?"

"He doesn't want me around the people doing time with him. He says they're dangerous, and they won't hesitate to use me against him."

It's tough surviving on the inside. Damian doesn't tell me what happens, but one of my friends dated a warden. The stories she told me gave me nightmares.

"Wise guy." He takes the glass from me and leaves it on the coffee table. "A prison full of hard, unscrupulous men is definitely not a place for a beautiful, young woman."

"Damian is innocent." I look into Maxime's cool gaze. "He didn't deserve that sentence. Whatever you think he did, he didn't do it."

"How can you be so sure?"

"He told me. I believe him. I *know* Damian. He didn't steal that diamond. Someone planted it on him."

"What kind of contact do you have? Do you call?"

"He says the phones are bugged. I write."

He lifts a brow. "Letters aren't monitored?"

"Damian knows the wardens in charge of reading the letters. They're safe. Besides, I don't share personal information."

"What do you write about, then?"

"My job." I shrug. "Everyday life."

"You mean your lack of a life."

My cheeks heat with more helpless anger. "You're an asshole."

"If you're so close, why doesn't he take care of his little sister?"

I glare at him. "How is he supposed to do that from a jail cell? Besides, I'm capable of taking care of myself."

He casts a glance around the room. "I've noticed."

"Times are hard for everyone." Dragging my gaze over his expensive suit, I add, "Well, not everyone. The thugs seem to thrive."

"Don't be so defensive, and it'll be wise to watch your tone with me. Do I need to remind you of the consequences of bad behavior?"

Tears choke me up when I think about Bruce. My answer is bitter. "No."

"Has Damian mentioned his plans for after his release?"

"He still has six of the ten-year-sentence to go." My heart hurts when I say it. "What plans can he make?"

"He never told you anything about acquiring a mine?"

"Are you joking? A mine must cost millions."

"Billions." Almost absent-mindedly, he rubs the stray strand of my hair between his fingers. "Did Damian tell you about money making schemes he's running in jail?"

"No." Unease starts digging into my gut. "Why? What is he involved in?"

He drops my hair. "Nothing. Just checking. Have you met any of his fellow inmates?"

"I told you, he doesn't want me to."

"Does the name Zane da Costa ring a bell?"

"He's Damian's cellmate, but that's all I know."

Getting up, he extends a hand. "I think you're telling the truth, but I'd like to see his letters."

I let him pull me to my feet. "There are no letters. Damian never writes back."

"Why not?"

"The wardens who read the outgoing letters aren't the same ones in charge of incoming mail. Damian doesn't trust them. He doesn't like them to know about my existence."

"What about photos? You must have some more of your brother."

I don't want to give him more information he can use against Damian. I don't want him to witness our poverty growing up. "Those are private."

"Zoe." He cups my cheek. "You need to understand that the only choices you have from now on are the ones I give you. I advise you to make those choices carefully. Don't waste them, because you'll have little enough. More importantly, don't test me. I'm not a patient man."

Gripping his wrist, I move his hand away. "Don't touch me."

His lips curve into a lazy smile. "I have a feeling you're going to swallow those words."

"Never," I say through clenched teeth.

"We'll see." He points at the hallway. "Get a move on."

I hurry away from him as fast as I can, but he follows close on my heel down the short hallway and into the room I once shared with my three brothers. Opening the dresser drawer, I take out the box of old photos and hand them to him. Doing so guts me, because those rare moments of our lives captured on film aren't meant for his hateful, emotionless eyes.

"Thank you," he says, accepting the box.

"I've given you what you want. Let Bruce go."

"What's Bruce to you?" He says the name with disdain.

"A kind neighbor." My look is accusing. "He's only ever been watching out for me."

"There's nothing romantic between you?"

I cross my arms. "No, not that it's any of your business."

"Do I need to remind you of your place?"

I avert my eyes, resenting him for taking my power. "You got what you wanted. Please, go."

"I'm not here for the photos."

Sick with fear, I look back at him. "What more do you want? You said you'd let us go."

"I never said that."

I take several steps back until my body hits the wall. "Did you lie? Are you going to kill us?"

"No."

"What then?" My whole body is shaking. Even the hem of my skirt is trembling.

"First things first. We're going out for dinner." His gaze drops to my gaping blouse again. "Make yourself presentable."

I stare at him. "Dinner?"

"You know," his tone is dry, "the meal you have between seven and nine."

"I have to go see Bruce," I exclaim. "He's hurt."

He opens the top drawer of my dresser and starts going through it. "He'll survive."

Dashing forward, I grab his arm. "Hey! What are you doing?"

He stops and looks at where I'm touching him.

I loosen my fingers and remove my hand. "That's mine, and it's private."

He sweeps aside my underwear and socks and checks underneath my sweater. He does the same with every drawer, and then pulls away the curtain to check inside the closet.

Without another word, he walks from the room and goes through the broom closet in the hallway before searching the closet in my late parents' room.

Satisfied that there's nothing of interest, he pulls out his phone. "We're leaving in five. This is one of those precious choices I'm allowing you, Zoe. You can either fix your clothes, or we go as you are."

"If I go with you, will you let Bruce go?"

"You're not in a position to bargain. You *are* coming with me, but don't worry about your neighbor. My business isn't with him."

Lifting the phone to his ear, he asks for a table for two while making his way back to the lounge. My chest is tight and my breathing shallow. Who *is* this arrogant man? What does he want? Is Damian in trouble? Is Bruce all right?

My tears are useless, but they flow anyway. Slipping into the bathroom, I lock the door. The window is too small to climb through. There's no backdoor. I'm trapped in my apartment with a dangerous man, a foreigner with cruel eyes and unknown intentions, but Bruce is even worse off.

I stare at my face in the mirror. I'm a mess. My mascara is smeared under my eyes. The neat bun of this morning is partly undone, my hair wild. I open the tap and rinse my face, washing away the mascara. The pins drop to the floor as I undo my hair with shaky fingers. I don't bother to pick them up. My brush is on the table in the lounge, and I'm not going there because *he* is there. Using my fingers, I comb through my hair to tame the tangles. Both my spare blouses are in the wash. I get a safety pin from the box with my needles and thread and pin the edges of the blouse together as best as I can. It takes longer than what it should because of how much I'm shaking. By the time I'm done, a knock falls on the door.

"Open the door, Zoe."

For a fleeting moment, I consider not complying, but I can imagine how that will go. It won't take much to kick down the door, and Bruce will suffer again because of my resistance. With my heart in my throat, I turn the key, but I don't push down the handle. My brain refuses to obey the command. It takes me a moment to search for the courage, but before I find it, Maxime opens the door.

"Let's go." He takes my arm and leads me to the lounge.

The blond man must've been standing just outside, because Maxime only has to knock once before the door is unlocked. When Maxime drags me through it, I know my life as I knew it has ended.

CHAPTER 2

Zoe

A black Mercedes with tinted windows is parked in the alley around the corner. It's new—judging by its shiny and flawless exterior—and a target for hijackers.

I glare at the blond guard as he opens the backdoor for Maxime who shoves me inside. Immune to my hostility, the blond gets behind the wheel while the bearded guy takes the passenger seat in the front. Unlucky for me, I share the backseat with the devil.

There's ample space, but he takes up all of it, making me shift into the corner against the door. His energy envelops me like a shadow eating up light until only the darkness of his intentions is left. The cologne that overwhelmed my senses since the moment he took me is more prominent in the confines of the car. He smells of cloves and citrus, a faint mix of winter that matches the cold color of his eyes and the frost that never melts in their depths.

The driver starts the engine while the bald one watches the road like a soldier looking out for danger in enemy territory. When the car pulls away, I twist around to look at my building. There's no movement behind Bruce's window.

Sagging back in my seat, I ask, "What do you want from me?"

Maxime doesn't answer. He's taken out his phone and is typing something.

The luxury car is so out of place in this suburb pedestrians slow down to stare. However, crime is nothing new. Women are kidnapped all the time. I won't be the first person to disappear from Brixton.

Has the driver locked the doors? Locals do it habitually, but my kidnappers are foreigners. There's a chance they might not have activated the central locking system.

It's rush hour. We're moving slowly. I have to take my chance while Maxime's attention is on his phone. By now Bruce would've alarmed someone. Hopefully, he's on his way to a hospital. Maxime can't hurt him anymore. Taking a shaky breath, I prepare myself for hitting the tarmac.

Now!

I yank the door handle.

It's locked.

Fuck.

"No," I moan, fresh tears welling up in my eyes.

Panic overwhelms me anew. My mind knows it's futile, but my body acts on survival instinct, demanding I try harder. Pulling with all my might, I shake the handle in a fit of hysteria.

A strong, warm hand folds over mine. I look down to where my kidnapper's fingers are curled around my fist, stilling me with minimal effort. His grip is firm without being too tight. I have no doubt he can easily crush my bones.

His voice is calm, a controlling force in the madness raging in my chest. "Look at me, Zoe."

I only comply because I don't know what he'll do if he loses his cool.

He regards me with those flat, frank eyes. "It'll be easier for both of us if you calm down."

The driver looks at me in the rearview mirror. He's clutching the wheel hard. His friend has one hand on the gun in his holster. I take it all in, jumping to the obvious conclusions.

"Over here." The clicking of Maxime's fingers draws my gaze. He's pointing at his face. "Eyes on me. That's better."

To my utter shame, my lip starts to wobble. "Are you going to kill me?"

"No." Maxime squeezes my hand and places it in my lap. "Why would I feed you if I was going to kill you? I already told you, I don't want to hurt you."

But he will if I don't do what he wants. If he doesn't want to tell me what he wants, it must be bad. This isn't a random kidnapping. Maxime targeted me for a reason. It has something to do with Damian. Maxime knows who I am. He knows where I live. He knows I live alone. He waited for me, knowing at what time I'd be arriving home from work.

Oh, my God. "Have you been stalking me?"

His smile is as flat as his eyes, like soda that's lost its bubbles. "The old lady in your building was only too happy to tell me everything I wanted to know."

"Mrs. Smit?" I gasp.

"It's amazing what a cup of tea and a slice of cake can buy."

"That's disgusting. You used that poor old lady."

"At least I'm not a stalker."

"Great." I stare through the window. "That makes me feel so much better."

"Sarcasm doesn't become you."

I turn my head back to him. "Really? You're lecturing me on my attitude?"

Focused on his phone again, he says, "I'll lecture you whenever I deem it necessary."

"Bruce would've called the police by now. They'll be looking for your men." I glance at the two guards again, but their eyes are trained on the road.

"Not for the theft of a cellphone. Your police have enough murders to keep them busy."

"You stole his cellphone?" I cry out.

He lifts a shoulder. "Motive for the forced entry and assault."

"You bastard."

The lines around his eyes tighten. "This is the last time I'm going to warn you about your language."

"Bruce is innocent. He's not rich like you. He can't afford another phone. How can you be so cruel?"

He chuckles. "You haven't seen cruelty yet, little flower."

"This is Brixton, in case you haven't noticed."

"I've noticed," he replies in a dry tone.

Meaning, the man who is carrying me off is worse than the neighborhood I've been trying to escape my whole life. I can't help but laugh in a hysterical fit at the irony.

"Something funny?" he asks.

"My life."

"You'll feel better when you've eaten."

I snort.

He takes a packet of tissues from the side of the door and drops it in my lap. "Any allergies or food dislikes I need to know about?"

I'm not going to wipe my eyes on his tissues. I use the back of my hand instead. "Couldn't find that out, huh? Why, your power does have limits."

Gripping my jaw, he doesn't squeeze hard enough to hurt, but with enough force to let me feel the underlying threat. "If you went for your regular health checks, I would've known."

I jerk free. "Yeah, well, doctor visits cost money."

"We'll correct that shortly."

"Correct what?" My pulse jumps again. "Why?"

"Just focus on what's important now. I asked you a question."

"I'm not answering your questions any longer. By now Bruce is safe. You can't manipulate me by hurting him anymore." I lift my chin. "When you let me out of this car, I'll run. I'll scream. You can't just take me."

Cruel calculation flashes in his eyes as he leans closer, pressing me against the door. "Do you know what an easy target a man in jail is?"

He brushes his knuckles over my cheek. "You see, Zoe, a man behind bars is nothing but a sitting duck. One word from me and your brother is dead."

Tears blur my vision. I slap away his hand. "I don't believe you."

He gets out of my face, giving me space to breathe. "Zane works for me. That, my pretty flower, you better believe."

The punch hits me straight in the gut, because what I do know is that Damian loves his cellmate like a brother. I feel sick. I want to spit in Maxime's face.

"I'll only ask you one more time," he says. "Do you have allergies or is there any food you hate?"

I clench my hands in my lap. "I'm not a fussy eater, and I don't have allergies."

"Medication?"

I frown. "What?"

His harsh features are emphasized by the shadows playing over his face as we pass under the bridge. "Are you on any medication?"

I fumble with my sleeves, a nervous habit. "Why are you asking?"

"Alcohol is prohibited with some medications."

"No, nothing."

Glancing at my restless fingers, he folds his hand over mine. "In that case, I hope you'll let me order for you."

Normally, I'd take offense to anyone making my decisions, especially deciding what I should eat, but this situation is so far removed from normal it feels unreal. What feels too real is where he's touching me. I'm like a kid with a vicious dog, tensing up, waiting for the moment it's going to bite, but then he pulls his hand away. My chest expands with a breath.

After dropping the threat on Damian's life like a hand grenade in my lap, Maxime continues to work on his phone quietly.

I have to warn Damian.

I look at the passing landscape while scheming, noting the landmarks as we drive north. Since we were kids, Damian and I had a secret code language. Our code words for trouble at home were apple pie.

I'll get word to Damian. I'll warn him Zane isn't his friend.

My turbulent thoughts are cut short when we stop at Seven Seas in Sandton. Only the wealthy and famous eat here. My monthly salary won't even cover a starter. I've seen pictures, but the private mansion converted into a restaurant is much more imposing in real life. The modern double story building is encased almost entirely in glass and situated on a vast, green lawn.

The blond guy opens my door. Ignoring his proffered hand, I get out. Maxime comes around to take my arm and steer me to the entrance. I can't help but stare at the lights in the double story foyer when we enter. A modern chandelier reaches all the way from the top level to the ground floor in a cascade of golden bulbs.

A hostess bustles over. "Max." She kisses his cheeks before taking his jacket. "Welcome back."

I suppress the urge to push the toe of my shoe into the carpet to hide the scruff where the color has worn off.

Her gaze flickers over me. "No bag for the lady?"

From her red Balenciaga number, it's obvious my antique lace blouse and mermaid skirt don't fit here, but I made them, and I love them.

Maxime lays a hand on my shoulder. "No bag."

His palm burns through the thin silk lining of the blouse. When the hostess turns away, I shake his touch off.

After putting Maxime's jacket in the cloakroom, she leads us down a red carpet to a veranda overlooking a fishpond that stretches the whole length of the lawn. A fountain with a sea snake spouting water from a forked tongue stands in the middle. Lilies drift on the water. It reminds me of an illustration of The Frog Prince in a book I owned, only this is no fairytale. I've stepped right into a nightmare.

Not having a choice, I sit down in the chair Maxime pulls out for me. A waiter drapes a linen napkin over my lap and hands me a menu. It's all very pretty and fancy, but I hate the place. We've entered a different world where unfamiliar rules and manners apply, a world where someone takes your jacket and judges you for the price tag on your clothes. Several other diners in eveningwear cast curious glances my way. With his European style, Maxime fits right in. I must stand out like the underprivileged kid in the candy store.

When Maxime opens his menu, I do the same, not because I'm eager to participate in this charade, but to block out his hateful face behind the big leather folder. There are no prices on mine. Going through the list of entrées and main courses, I understand why Maxime suggested ordering for me. It wasn't so much a gesture of control than saving me the embarrassment of admitting I understand nothing. The dishes all have foreign names. I'm guessing they're French. There's nothing I recognize.

The waiter returns with appetizers. "Sea urchin on Melba toast with truffle oil."

I stare at the disc of bread with a dollop of red cream, a sprig of chive, and three dots of oil on the side.

"Do you like urchin?" Maxime asks.

"I don't know." Isn't it's obvious I can't afford food like this? "I've never had it."

"Some people love it. Others hate it. Go ahead. Try it."

I haven't eaten since breakfast, but I don't have an appetite. Even if I were starving, which technically I am, I would've declined on principle. I'm not selling my soul to the devil for a meal.

I push the plate away. "No, thanks."

His eyes crinkle in the corners, but the set of his mouth is hard. "I'll feed you if you prefer." He pronounces the words carefully in his accent, making sure I understand. "On my lap."

He'll do it. I have no doubt. He's callously uncaring about how people are looking at us, or rather at me. Defeated, I give him a cutting look as I take the morsel between two fingers and place it in my mouth. It's salty and smoky with a strong but not off-putting iodine aftertaste.

"Do you like it?" he asks.

I cross my arms. "No."

"I'll order you something more ordinary, then."

The insult is payback for my ungrateful and bad-mannered reply, but I couldn't care less. Yes, I'm poor. Yes, I'm not used to much, certainly not urchin, and caviar, and whatever else they serve here, but at least I'm not a criminal who breaks into people's homes and kidnaps them.

Picking up the knife and fork on the far outside of his plate, Maxime scoops up the bite and brings it to his lips. I want to crawl under the table for demonstrating just how uneducated I am by eating with my hands. It's not that I care what he or the people around us think. I just hate giving them the pleasure of being right about me.

The waiter returns with a bottle of wine and pours us each a glass, after which he takes our order. Maxime has no problem pronouncing the names of the dishes.

When the waiter is gone, I decide to go for a blunt approach. I already know my kidnapper's name. Knowing less or more about him won't make a difference in my fate.

"Are you French?" I ask.

His lips quirk in one corner. "What gave me away?"

"Your accent."

"It was a rhetorical question, Zoe. It's called humor."

Some of the fear makes place for anger. "Don't patronize me."

"I wasn't patronizing you." His smile grows into a full, mocking curve. "I was just pointing out the obvious."

I hate him. He did this on purpose, making me feel stupid for asking. Not wanting to talk to him anymore, I turn my head away.

"Why so angry, my little Zoe? Is it because I didn't fall for your transparent way of fishing for information about me?"

I look back at him. "I'm not your little Zoe, and actually, I brought it up because your accent is rather unpleasant on the ear."

He raises a brow. "Is that so?"

I'm not going to tell him he makes talking sound like sex. I bet that's what he's used to hearing.

"Strange," he drawls. "You're the first woman to complain."

"Oh, I'm sorry." I bat my eyelashes. "Did I hurt your fragile ego?"

"No teacher ever managed to rid me of this accent, no matter how many private tutors I had."

There's honesty in that statement, like an olive branch he's offering. I'm too desperate to know why he took me not to take it. "You speak English well enough."

He takes a sip of wine. "A business requirement."

"What kind of business are you in?" I can't stop myself from adding, "Human trafficking?"

He only smiles broader. "When necessary."

The waiter arrives with our starters. It looks like some kind of seafood soup. In different circumstances, the spicy aroma would've made my mouth water, but my stomach churns when the waiter puts a bowl down in front of me.

"Bisque," Maxime says. "I hope you'll like it."

I stare at the lobster tail drifting in the center of the bowl.

"The secret is in the sherry," he says, bringing his spoon to his mouth.

I drag my gaze from the bowl to his face. "So, France is home."

"Eat your food, Zoe. If you need to know something, I'll tell you."

My anger escalates. "Ah, so we're on a need-to-know basis."

"Exactly."

"What about after dinner? What happens then?"

He stills. "You really need to live more in the present, to enjoy the moment."

"Because something bad is going to happen later?" I ask a little louder.

His gaze hardens. "Keep your voice down and eat your food."

If I eat one bite, I'm going to vomit. "I'm not hungry."

"I'm not feeding you again until tomorrow morning."

The last two words get stuck in my head. *Tomorrow morning.* They add to my barely controlled panic. "Why do you need me until the morning? Why are you doing this?" He reaches over the table for my hand, but I pull away. "Tell me. Tell me now."

"Calm down. I don't want to embarrass you in front of all these people by teaching you your place."

"On your lap?" I say in a catty tone.

"*Over* my lap, and then you'll eat *on* my lap with a smarting ass."

Tears that refuse to dry up burn behind my eyes. "I hate you."

"I know. You'll hate me even more if Damian gets a beating tonight." He motions with his spoon at my untouched soup. "Now eat."

"I can't. I'll be sick."

He wipes his mouth on his napkin. "You have two choices. You can either eat the delicious food and enjoy the conversation or be treated like a child and go to bed hungry and sulking. You can see why the first option is hands down the winner. You'll nourish your body and make the best of a moment you don't have any control over. It's up to you. Just know I won't hesitate to execute my threat. I don't make idle ones."

I'm crying with helpless anger by the time his speech is done. I don't even care any longer that everyone is staring. I just want to go home.

"What will it be, Zoe?"

Picking up my spoon, I grip it so hard the metal pushes painfully into my palm.

"Good decision." His voice is calm but his gaze attentive, waiting for the moment I crack.

I dunk the spoon with a shaking hand in my bowl. The tremors running over my body are no longer only from fear, but also from anger and injustice. I force the liquid down my throat, tasting nothing.

Maxime continues to watch me until I've cleared my bowl. Every swallow is a battle I fight. I drink more wine than I'm used to, downing the first glass and throwing back another straight after.

The waiter doesn't look at me as he clears our bowls and serves the main dish—lobster for Maxime and *ordinary* pasta for me. I somehow manage to eat everything and keep it down, although in the morning I'll probably not even remember what I ate.

Through it all, Maxime makes conversation and even lighthearted jokes. When our dessert and herbal tea arrive, he pours a cup and hands it to me.

"What do you do at the sweatshop?" he asks.

"I'm a seamstress."

His gaze drops to my blouse. "Did you make that?"

"Yes."

"I didn't notice a sewing machine in your apartment."

"I use the machines at work."

"Doesn't the manager have a problem with that?"

"The supervisor lets us use them after hours."

He brings the cup to his lips. "Is that what you always wanted to do?"

"It's a steppingstone."

"To designing."

I nod. He saw the books on my bookshelf.

"Honey?" He pushes the pot toward me.

"No." I take sugar, but I don't say so.

"You're talented."

I shrug.

The conversation continues in this manner until he asks for the bill. He pays with a stack of cash that would've covered my rent for a couple of months. He asks if I need to use the bathroom and waits outside the door until I'm done.

The guards are smoking in the garden. They put out their cigarettes when we approach. The blond one hurries to get my door, but Maxime waves him away.

"I've got this, Gautier."

Once inside, Maxime turns to me. "Would you like to go for a drink somewhere, maybe show me another part of your city?"

I rub my temples where a headache is building. "I've played your game. I've eaten my food. I just want to go home."

"As you wish," he says, "but you're not going home."

My body goes rigid. "Where am I going?"

He nods at Gautier, who pulls off as Maxime says, "To my hotel."

CHAPTER 3

Maxime

Glass skyscrapers and modern office blocks dominate the view as we drive to my hotel in Melrose Arch. It's nothing like the crumbling buildings and weed-infested pavements of Zoe Hart's suburb. I've seen worse neighborhoods. In my line of work, there's always worse. Yet for some reason, the empty buildings with planks crossed over their broken windows in Brixton made me tense. We're armed with enough weapons to defend ourselves should anyone be stupid enough to attack us, but it's not my safety I fear. The uneasiness eating at me is for the woman I just found and can't afford to lose. Her apartment doesn't even have an alarm, for God's sake.

In a place like that, it's only a matter of time before she turns into a statistic. The fact that I'll be the one to turn her into that statistic doesn't faze me, which says a lot about the kind of man I am.

I regard my petite charge. She's quiet now, her worry bigger than her anger. It's not that I don't want to put her at ease. It's just that I can't tell her the truth. Her hands are clutched together in her lap.

Every now and then, she untangles those long, slender fingers to rub at a temple. That should teach her for downing two glasses of the most expensive wine in the restaurant without even tasting it. Not that I blame her.

She's right to be nervous. She should be wary of me. I'm angry with her, even if it's not her fault. I'm angry that she put me in this position, a position that makes me give a damn. How could I not look at her as a person after going through her apartment and witnessing the dreams so obviously strewn around? She wears them like the emotions in her expressive eyes—on her sleeve. Hope shines in those wide blue irises, and hope makes a person human.

The problem is I've never dealt with an innocent. Everyone in my business has dirt on his hands, but Zoe is only a pawn. If I hand her over to my younger brother, as planned, she'll be broken and nothing but a shell of herself, those beautiful dreams and naïve hope crushed and forgotten by the time we send her back to her brother. If we ever do.

I had to drive the last woman unfortunate enough to have ended up in Alexis's bed to hospital. Her injuries weren't pretty. Even without the payoff from my father, she wouldn't have pressed charges. The consequences are too terrifying. Our family is feared. It's not fair, but that's life for you.

Zoe tenses more when we pull up at the hotel. Part of her fault is that she's pretty and exactly Alexis's type. He'll like her dark hair and pale skin. He'll want her. That makes her my problem, one I don't need and shouldn't want. Yet I do. Maybe that's the real problem. I've wanted her since I pressed her body against mine and slammed my hand over her mouth.

I liked the head rush I got from holding her in my power. I liked how clean her apartment was amidst the filth of the buildings surrounding hers. I liked the simple wildflower and the cherished green plant on her windowsill. Just like her. She's a pretty little daisy that pushes through a crack on a dirty pavement, resilient and beautiful, surviving against the odds.

She's poor as fuck, but she's proud. I like that, too. Judging by the books she reads and the clothes she fancies, she's a romantic. That, I like the most. It fascinates me. I want to know how she can believe in something so abstract and idyllic that doesn't exist. Even if it did, she certainly wouldn't have found it in Brixton.

I want to know how the fuck she can still believe in something beautiful, in anything at all, when everything around her is dilapidated, rotten, and hopeless. I want to know how someone with her fragile body and meager means survives. I want to know how her soul can crack concrete and flourish with no one's care to shine like a daisy amidst the grime. Maybe, just maybe, if I know her secret, I'll know how to be happy. Maybe if I can catch her spirit, I can steal her dreams and make her hope mine.

Zoe glances at me when we pull up at the hotel. She's been wringing her hands since we left the restaurant. Instead of quieting her fiddling, I let her have the outlet even if it distracts me from my thoughts of what the fuck to do with her. I get out and go around to get her door. I don't give her a chance to reject my offer to help her from the car like she did with Gautier. With him, I allowed it, preferred it even. I didn't like him touching her. My grip on her waist is firm as I swipe my access card to open the door and lead her inside. There's no receptionist or lobby staff, part of the reason why I chose to stay here. It's more like an aparthotel with the services of a hotel.

Gautier and Benoit scout the area before they follow, as much from habit as a necessity in a high crime area. We ride the elevator together. I tell them in French to have dinner before catching a few hours of sleep. It's only after eight. The kitchen staff deliver meals to the rooms until ten. We have a long day ahead of us tomorrow.

On the top floor, we split. They go to the room they share at the end while I take Zoe to the penthouse suite.

She pulls back when I unlock the door with my card, but it doesn't take much to push her over the threshold. She doesn't weigh more than a cat. A small kitten, really. When I lock the door, she puts distance between us, backtracking to the middle of the floor.

The suite is three times the size of Zoe's apartment. She looks lost, hugging her slight frame in the middle of the lounge in her frilly blouse and hip-hugging skirt, and even more petite than usual against the floor-to-ceiling window framing Melrose Arch. With those black curls and pearly skin, she's more than easy on the eye. Long lashes frame her blue eyes, and her mouth is pouty like a budding rose. The blush on her cheeks is as pink as the petals of that rose, the darker hue closer to the stem if I were to pull the flower apart.

At my evaluation, she folds into herself like a flower that curls up at night. I'm staring too openly, the lust I don't care to show in public probably visible on my face. I remove my jacket and hang it over the clotheshorse. Then I put my Glock and access card in the safe, making sure my body blocks the code so the little flower I plucked from her life isn't baited with temptation.

When I turn back to her, her eyes are swimming with trepidation. The way the tears make them glitter are gorgeous. They seem bigger and even more expressive. It's a pretty sight, but I don't want to torture her. She did nothing to deserve what's coming to her.

Folding back my shirt sleeves, I advance slowly so I won't frighten her. She tilts her head back to meet my gaze when I stop in front of her.

Her voice is as silky as her flower-petal skin. "Why am I here?"

I know what she's really asking. "Don't worry. I'm as little a rapist as I'm a stalker." Only a killer.

Swaying a little, she frowns and rubs at her temples. "Then why did you bring me to your hotel?"

She's exhausted, has been since she came home with sagging shoulders, dragging feet, and two tomatoes for dinner. "To sleep."

"I have a bed. I have a home."

Not any longer. I walk to the wet bar and pour a glass of water, which I carry back to her. "You had too much wine too quickly. Drink."

She takes the glass and gulps everything down. I refill it and take the pill from the box waiting next to the decanter. It's a good thing I had the foresight. Being kidnapped can be draining on all counts, both the spirit and the body.

"What is it?" she asks when I hand the pill to her with the water.

"Something for your headache."

She regards me with mistrust, as she should. It's not a lie. It will take away her pain. It's just not the full truth. It's not the first time I don't give her the truth, and it won't be the last.

"How did you know I have a headache?"

"It's obvious from the way you rub your temples."

She studies my face with wide, weary eyes. I see the exact moment she decides to believe me. Putting the pill in her mouth, she swallows it down with the water.

I take back the glass. "I have some business to take care of. Why don't you have a nice, warm bath?"

She glances at the bedroom door.

"This way." I take her arm and lead her to the opposite door that gives access to the bathroom. "I'll be a while. Take your time."

She looks around the room, seeming as lost as when I brought her into the suite.

"Do you need help with operating the facilities?"

Her look is scathing. "I can open a tap."

Ah, her fire hasn't burned out. It pleases me. I smile. "Call if you need me."

She scoffs before pushing past me and slamming the door in my face. The lock turns on the other side. As if she has any power. Grinning, I shake my head and drag a hand over my face. The stretch of my lips is a foreign feeling, something I haven't experienced in long time. Maybe never.

Leaving the little flower to her bath, I steel myself for the call I have to make. Certain she can't escape, I go onto the balcony for privacy and check the hour. It's the same time in France.

It takes a while for my father to take the call. From the cutlery sounding in the background, he's having dinner.

"Did I catch you at a bad time?" I ask in French.

It's my brother who replies. He's jovial, a few glasses of wine already in his stomach. "How are things working out in South Africa?"

I roll my shoulders, but my voice comes out tight, anyway. "Fine. I didn't know Maman invited you for dinner."

"We're at the club."

My spine goes stiff. The club is where the deals are made. Alexis is greedy to undermine my power. "Let me speak to our father."

"Do you have her?" He sounds excited.

Something dark stirs in my chest. I can't discuss her with him. Even that little will soil her.

"Max?" Alexis's voice rises in volume. "We have a bad connection. I can't hear you."

"Put Father on, Alexis. It's late."

He laughs. "Getting old?"

I let the jab slide, but get one of my own in. "Pronto, *little brother*."

The diminutive works. A moment later, my father's cigar-rough voice comes on the line. "Did you meet with Dalton?"

Good evening to you, too, Dad. "You're at the club."

"The business doesn't go on hold when you're not here."

I force nonchalance into my tone. "What's Alexis doing there?"

The way my father changes from brusque to overly friendly tells me everything I want to know. "It's just dinner, Max."

"I thought you said it's business."

"For me. Your brother is networking. Enough of family. Tell me about Harold Dalton. Did you see him?"

"Last night." I hated every minute of the dinner I shared with that shark.

"And?"

"He's not going to last."

There's a moment of silence. "Is he as bad as our dealers say?"

"Worse. His mine reeks of mismanagement, and his board is corrupt."

"Did you have a look at the books?"

"Only the ones he wanted me to see. He did a good job of trying to hide it, but they're definitely cooked." I have a nose for figures. It only takes me a moment to know when one and one don't add up to two.

"I see." Another short silence. "In that case, we won't interfere with Damian Hart's scheme."

"I'll advise against it. From looking at all the facts, Hart is the best man to revive that mine. Plus, his motivation is personal." *Personal* always guarantees the best results.

"Then we let Dalton go under when the time comes."

"In two years' time, we won't be making any more money out of him. He's running the mine into the ground."

Literally.

Harold Dalton is the owner of one of the most lucrative diamond mines in South Africa. He sells to us directly, cutting out the brokers and wholesalers, which earns us a big fat saving of thirty percent. When you're talking billions, thirty percent is a considerable chunk, enough to bribe and, if needed, kill for.

Word has it that the mine is running empty and will soon go bankrupt. We keep a close ear on the ground. In our business, it's imperative. We have informants everywhere, even in Dalton's mining workforce, and we're not the only ones who play that game.

It turns out Damian Hart has informants, too. He knows about the mine's pending failure. According to his cellmate and our informant, Zane da Costa, the mine has unyielded potential that Dalton is too thick in the head to exploit. Da Costa sold us information about Hart's plans to take over the mine when he gets out of jail. According to Hart, Dalton stole his discovery, and he has every intention of taking it back.

From what I've learned about his strategy and how he's planning on going about it, my money is on Hart. For the time being, Dalton is giving us the first buying option for a kickback. Hart wants to bring back the wholesalers and cut out the shady dealers like ourselves, which poses a problem for our business. If Hart takes away thirty percent of our business, everything will fold—the casinos, shipping companies, our whole empire. Our mission is ensuring Hart honors the deal, and for that to happen, we need a sword we can hold over Hart's head.

My father sighs. "I hate change. Too damn unpredictable."

At least that's one thing we agree on. "Better the devil you know."

"I take it you found Hart's sister."

Dipping a finger into the knot of my tie, I loosen it. "Why else would I call?"

"Are they as close as da Costa said?"

"I don't doubt it." If I had a sister like Zoe, I'd protect her with my life.

"Good. Bring her in."

I hesitate. "It'll take some time." With enough time, I could let her become used to me and even brainwash her into believing it was her idea to leave.

Impatience infuses his tone. "Tomorrow."

"Why the rush?"

"Business is like a game of chess, son. You've got to have your pieces in place before your opponent has as much as thought about moving his. I'm not taking any chances. It'll be checkmate before Hart even enters the game."

"We have six years before Hart has served his sentence. He's only starting to gain power in jail."

A glass clinks. It's time for my father's after-dinner cognac. "I heard from da Costa. Hart may be released from prison early for good behavior."

"How early?"

"In two years."

Someone on the outside is paying Hart for services rendered on the inside. He doesn't have access to that money yet, but in two years' time he'll be considerably wealthier. With wealth comes power, which is the second reason we're not taking him out. Number one is he has the ability to revive a mine that sustains our business, and number two is he's wasted no time in making powerful allies in jail. Some of the families who run Hart's country and pull the politician's strings have members on the inside. They're not the kind of enemies we want or can afford to make.

"How sure are you of this informant?" I've always had a bad feeling about the rat.

"Nothing is ever sure, but this one is power hungry."

They're the easiest to buy, the ones without honor or loyalty.

My father exhales. I imagine him sucking on his cigar. "Let me know at what time you'll arrive."

Staring at the city lights, I consider this new dilemma I didn't expect. I consider what I'm going to do, telling myself it hasn't crossed my mind even once. "Expect me back after the weekend, not before."

"Why the delay?" my father asks.

"I have loose ends to tie up."

Laughter sounds in the background.

"I've got to go," my father says. "The girls have arrived."

I clench my fists. My words are measured. "Say hello to Maman for me."

My father doesn't like the rebuke. The line goes dead. I stare at the phone in my hand. Fuck. If I had more time—

"Maxime?"

I turn around.

Zoe stands in the open sliding door, barefoot and drowning in a hotel robe. Her dull eyes show the medication is kicking in. "What was that about?"

I pocket the phone. "Nothing that concerns you."

"It sounded like a fight."

"Go inside." My body is tense, my cock taking notice of how little there is between my hand and her skin. "You'll catch a cold."

"I don't feel well."

It's not a lie or an attempt at manipulation. The pill will do that. In a minute, she'll be a little nauseous, too.

I close the distance and take her arm. "You're tired. You'll feel better after you've rested."

"I need my clothes." Her tongue slurs a bit. "I have nothing to wear to bed."

In the room, I stop to take one of my T-shirts from the dresser. "Put that on. You can take the bed."

She watches me with drooping, albeit wary eyes. "What about you?"

"I'll take the couch."

"Okay," she says with obvious relief. She takes the T-shirt and stumbles on her way to the bed.

I catch her around the waist before she hits the floor. "I'm sorry, little flower." She smells like the hotel shampoo. When I first pressed her against me, her skin and hair smelled like roses. I make a mental note to get the same brand of shampoo I saw in her apartment before we go.

Helping her into a sitting position on the bed, I stay close in case she pukes.

She puts a hand over her stomach. "I feel sick."

"You'll be fine."

Her long lashes lift, her eyes scanning my face with an ingrained desire to trust. "I think I ate something. The urchin maybe."

"There was nothing wrong with the food. Relax. It'll get better in a minute."

"May I please have some water?"

"Wait it out." I don't want her to puke up what's left of the pill in her stomach.

"Maxime?" There's panic in her sleep-heavy voice.

"Shh." I brace her nape with one hand and cup her cheek with the other, brushing my thumb over the soft skin under her eye as I watch them lose more focus until her eyelids finally close and unconsciousness takes her.

Gently, I lower her to the bed and take a step back. Her hair is spread out around her face, the curls framing her beautiful bone structure. My T-shirt is still in her hand, her dainty fingers folded around it softly. The robe gapes slightly where her legs are bent over the edge. I grow hard looking at her like this. I imagine stripping the robe and spreading her legs to watch her. I imagine dragging my hands over the contours of her body and getting to know her curves while she's out cold. The dark, invasive thought makes me even harder. I could tell her I had to dress her in the T-shirt, so she'd sleep more comfortably. She'd never know if I stroked her or stroked myself while looking at her.

But not like this.

My thoughts are sick. They make me sick.

Disgusted, I grab my testicles and squeeze until my eyes water. The pain is good. It grounds me. I deserved that.

I arrange her like a princess on the bed and cover her with the duvet. Then I sink down into the armchair with my head in my hands, watching, thinking. When I've decided, I get up. I'd like to watch her all night, but there's plenty to do.

It takes a lot of work to make a person disappear.

CHAPTER 4

Zoe

I wake up groggy. My throat is dry, and my eyes burn. I'm lying in a big bed, covered by a soft blanket, instead of on the lumpy mattress of my single bed. Memories from yesterday return, of a man with big hands and a winter's day eyes. I shoot upright.

Blinking, I look around the room, but it's not the hotel room from last night. Wait. What happened before I passed out? The last I recall was feeling sick. Maxime took me to the bedroom and gave me a T-shirt. After that, my mind is a blank.

I glance down at the hotel robe I'm wearing. No T-shirt. I don't remember putting it on or going to bed. My panic escalates as I survey the room with the Renaissance furniture and golden brocade curtains I don't remember.

Where am I?

Jumping from the bed, I rush to the window and yank the curtains open. The view makes me stumble a step back, gasping as I take in the dome roofs and towers over the canal.

My heart beats furiously as I turn back to the room for clues. My bare feet are quiet on the thick carpet as I run to the adjoining room and peer inside. It's a bathroom. I'm desperate, so I lock the door and use the facilities before washing my hands and splashing cold water on my face to clear my head.

The bathroom is even bigger than the one of last night. The shower has twin nozzles. A spa bath window overlooks more sandstone buildings and cobblestone streets. I run to the window and check for a handle, but there isn't one. It doesn't open. Light streams into the room, the sun still high. It's sometime in the morning, maybe around ten.

I go back into the room and open the closet. It's empty. I check the nightstand for stationary or a complimentary pen, any clue, but there's nothing. I have a terrible suspicion, one so unreal it's absurd to even think it. I hurry to the other door and push the handle down. It opens onto a lounge as luxuriously decorated as the bedroom. Maxime sits in an armchair, a cup of espresso on the coffee table. He stands when I enter. Dressed in a dark suit and silver tie, he's as impeccably groomed as yesterday.

"Where am I?" I cry out, going to the lounge window. The view over the square is strangely familiar, yet I know this isn't home. This isn't South Africa.

"Calm down, Zoe. Come have breakfast, and I'll explain."

I spin around. "I don't want breakfast."

He walks to a table and lifts the silver lid from one of the dishes. A waft of pancakes fills the air. He points at the chair. "Please."

The word is a command. Not hungry in the least, I pad over cautiously and lower myself into the seat. He adjusts my chair and serves two pancakes on the plate in front of me before reaching for a bowl of cream.

I can't stand it. I have to know. "Did you touch me?"

His hand stills on the serving spoon. It's minute, but I notice. He drops a dollop on each pancake. "No."

I don't know if I believe him, but he definitely didn't rape me. I would've felt the difference in my body, wouldn't I? "What's going on? Please tell me where we are."

Offering me a bowl of strawberries, he waits with an outstretched arm. It's clear he's not going to budge until I serve myself. I take a strawberry without paying attention to what I'm doing. I'm too focused on his face, looking for answers.

He pours tea that smells like roses into a porcelain cup and puts it next to my plate before taking the seat opposite me. "We're in Venice."

The strawberry drops from my fingers. It rolls over the carpet under the table. I can feel the blood drain from my face as he gives me the verbal confirmation of what I suspected.

"Why?" I whisper.

"I thought you wanted to come here."

He saw the books in my apartment. I clench my jaw. He stole me. That's terrifying, but somehow this, the fact that he invaded my dreams, feels so much worse.

"Eat," he says. "You need your strength."

I grab the knife. The shaft shakes in my hand. Am I capable of stabbing him? Can I drive the blunt end into his black, devious heart? "How did I get here?"

"I have a plane."

"You abducted me." I can't make sense of the facts staring me in the eyes. "I don't even have a passport."

"You didn't. You do now."

"How…You can't just get a passport overnight."

He doesn't answer.

Oh, my God. He came prepared. He came to South Africa with a passport. My kidnapping was well thought out. Premeditated. "Just tell me what you want."

He crosses his legs as he considers me with his emotionless eyes. Does he even feel anything? Is he a psychopath? His face is rough and unsightly to look at, but it's the flatness of those sharp, gray eyes that scares me the most.

"Eat," he says again, "and then we'll talk."

I eat, not because I want to, but so he'll tell me what's going on. The pancakes are fluffy, but I don't taste anything.

"Have a strawberry," he says. "They're out of season. I had them flown in especially."

I stare at the bowl of fat, red strawberries. Each one is perfect, almost too pretty to be real. Taking one, I bite into the flesh. Juice runs over my chin. I catch it with my palm. He reaches over the table, offering me a linen napkin. I snatch it from his hand, scrunching it up in my fist before dumping it next to my plate in an impulsive act of defiance.

The warm drink is the only thing I really want. I reach for the tea. "I ate. Now talk."

Rubbing a thumb over his lips, he seems to weigh his words. After an awkward silence, he says, "We need to borrow you for a while."

The warm tea scalds my throat as I almost choke on the sip I took. "Borrow me? We?"

"My family."

I replace the cup on the saucer lest I drop the hot liquid in my lap. "What for?"

"You don't need to concern yourself over the details. What you need to know is Damian's life is in your hands."

Shock runs through me. He—they—intend to keep me. If I don't comply, Damian will pay. "I have a job, a home, friends—"

"You resigned," he says. "I already gave up your lease and took care of your outstanding bills."

"You can't do that," I exclaim. "My plant… the cats… nobody else will feed them."

"Your neighbor kindly took your plant, and I'm paying for the food he'll feed the cats. He also promised to return your library books."

I jump to my feet. "You went back to see Bruce?"

"He sent a text to your phone to tell you what happened. He wisely thought he should warn you about the thieves targeting your building. I explained you were with me and wanted me to check on him."

"You told him I was going away with you. Is that the lie you told him?"

"He was happy for you. Oh, and you'll also be glad to know I replaced his phone. He was very grateful for the gesture."

I swallow down my tears. I can't believe this is happening. "You drugged me."

"It was easier that way, less stressful for you."

I curl my hands into balls at my sides. "You don't know what's easier for me."

"Sit down and finish breakfast. We have work to do before I can show you the city."

"You want to go fucking sightseeing?"

"Mind your tongue, Zoe. We're really going to have to do something about your language."

"Is that why you brought me here?" Every muscle in my body is trembling in rage. "As payoff for *borrowing* me?"

"No," he says softly. "Not for that."

"How long exactly is this borrowing supposed to last?"

"Three, four years. It's hard to say. It all depends."

Four years? I place a hand over my stomach, feeling sick again. "On what?"

"I can't say."

His calm indifference infuriates me. I want to slap him. Kill him. My gaze darts to the teapot. If I throw it into his face—

"Don't even think about it," he says. "Gautier and Benoit are right outside. I really don't want to punish you, but I will. I'm not going to threaten you with Damian again. The next time you disobey me, I'll put those threats into action." He gets up and walks over, stopping close to me. "This," he waves an arm around the room, "is not going to happen every day, maybe never again, so I suggest you make the most of it. Enjoy the food. Enjoy the trip. I went to a lot of effort and spent a lot of money to make this happen for you. Whether you hate it or set aside your pride to enjoy it won't change your fate. You may as well make the wise choice and make the most of it."

With his speech done, he watches me with a raised brow, waiting for me to make my decision. I want to fling myself at him in a fit of fury and punch him in his ugly face, but I can't surrender to my anger. That's not an option he gave me, not unless I want to suffer the consequences of getting my brother hurt. The wiser option is to tamp down my bitter anger and mad rage, and to obey like a dog.

It takes all the strength I possess to sit back down and fold my hands around the teacup. It hurts. It hurts my self-esteem and my pride, but I swallow it with my tears, not only for Damian, but also for myself.

"Good decision," he says, squeezing my shoulder.

My body stiffens under his touch. Thankfully, he pulls his hand away.

While I force pancakes and strawberries down my throat, washing it down with rose petal tea, he makes phones calls in French. He stays on the far side of the lounge, as if giving me space would help to keep down my food.

When my plate is empty, he calls me over with a flick of his fingers.

I stand and walk over like the obedient dog he's making of me.

Approval softens his features. He likes my obedience, or maybe it's just easier for him not having to fight and threaten me constantly. "Would you like to have a shower? I'm having clothes sent over for you in a while."

"I have clothes." Which I love.

"They won't serve you here."

I give him a hateful look.

His smile is patient. "The weather here is much less forgiving than in your country."

"I'll have a shower," I bite out.

"Another good choice." Another mocking smile. "You'll find everything you need in the bathroom."

I go to the bathroom and lock the door for good measure. As he promised, the cabinet is stocked with cosmetics and toiletries. I even find my normal brand of shampoo as well as the conditioner I could never afford.

Opting for the shower instead of the bath, I quickly wash and dry off. I apply some body lotion to alleviate the dryness of my skin. I don't know if it's a side effect of the drugs or the flight. I've never travelled. I do know from reading that Venice is a fourteen-hour-long flight from Johannesburg. The surrealism of it all still shakes me to my core. When I'm done, I pull on a clean robe with a hotel logo.

Maxime is waiting in the lounge when I step out. There's a rail with dresses, jackets, and coats. Several pairs of boots are displayed on the floor. A box with underwear stands on the coffee table.

"I think this is your size," he says.

Despite my resolution to take as little from Maxime as possible, I can't help but go over to admire the clothes. My fingers itch to touch the fabric. I lift a tag and nearly faint at the price. It's Valentino. I've never shopped in a department store, let alone a boutique. My clothes are either self-made or bought at the flea market. Owning a piece from a world-renowned designer has only featured in my dreams, which is why I drop the tag. I'm not giving Maxime more of my dreams.

"What's wrong?" he asks. "Don't you like the clothes?"

I turn to face him. "No."

He shrugs. "Then I'll choose what you wear."

I watch with mounting anger as he takes a navy wool dress with white sailor collar and matching coat from the rail.

"I think this will look good on you." He pushes the items into my hands. "Go put that on."

I jut out my chin. "No."

"You prefer to go out naked?" Something sparks in his eyes, something dark and demented, as if the idea appeals to him. "Maybe I should let you walk around without clothes. I could put a collar and chain on you instead. Would you like that? Would the way people look at you make you wet?"

"You're sick," I spit out.

He puts his nose inches from mine. "Right now you still have a choice. Remember what I said about not wasting the little you have."

Dumping the blue set on the couch, I back away. "Fine. You win. You can have your way in this, but you'll never have a piece of my soul."

He smiles. "I never asked for your soul."

Seething, I spin away from him and flip through the clothes with more force than necessary. My hand stills on a beautiful pink coat with a scrunched collar. The matching dress is a fitted cut with puffy sleeves.

"Good choice," he says.

Grabbing the box with the underwear, I escape to the room. The dress fits perfectly. I finish off the outfit with nude winter tights and boots.

A knock falls on the door just as I finish drying my hair. I pull a brush through it and reluctantly open the door.

Maxime's gaze trails over me. There's nothing in his eyes to tell me what he thinks, not that I care.

"Time for work." He takes my hand and pulls me into the lounge.

I jerk free but follow him to the writing desk pushed against a window. A writing block with the hotel logo and pen lie on the desk. He pulls out the chair in silent command. Once I'm seated, he puts the pen in my hand.

"You're going to write a letter," he says.

I already know before I ask, "To who?"

"To Damian. You're going to tell him you met someone, a foreigner visiting your country, and that he swept you off your feet. Love at first sight. You went out for dinner. It was beautiful, like a fairytale. You were devastated when he had to go back to his country. He couldn't bear leaving you behind, so he asked you to come with him. You didn't think twice. He got you a passport, and you left the country. You're in Europe with him now, and you're very, very happy."

He presses his palms on the desk, putting our faces close together. His eyes are cold, as always, but it's a different kind of cold, a cold that frightens me, because flames can burn a cold shade of winter.

"So happy, that you're never going back."

It's that spark flickering under the deepest layers of gray ash that makes me lean back. It's the story he told, the one he stole from my books that parts my lips on a soundless gasp. It punches a hole straight through my heart, because this will be the most terrible lie I've ever told, and I've never lied to my brother, not even once.

My nostrils stir in the stare-off between us, faint tremors running over my body and accumulating in my fingers where he pushed the pen.

I was holding out for that story, for that love. That man. He has no right to steal that place, to take my fantasy and twist it into a hopeless lie. I can't write it. If I do, I'll lose a piece of myself, and I swore I wouldn't.

The pen drops from my fingers. It rolls to the edge of the desk where he catches it.

I shake my head. "I can't."

He puts the pen back in my hand, folding my fingers around it. "You will."

"I'll come up with something." My voice is hoarse. "Something Damian will believe."

"He'll believe this." He pushes a strand of hair behind my ear. "Nothing else."

How does this stranger know so much about me from going through my belongings? There's more to this than cooking up a believable story. Maxime wants to make my fantasy his own. He wants to feature in it. That's what those cold flames signify —excitement.

"I've never lied to my brother," I say in a feeble attempt to appeal to his compassion, even if I'm starting to believe he has none.

"I wouldn't corrupt you if I had a choice." His gaze moves to my lips, then to the neckline of the dress. "In this, there is no choice."

He says it with so much conviction, regret almost, that I'm silent for a moment. The statement is false. Of course, he has a choice, but he believes he doesn't. I want to beg him not to make me do it, but he tightens his fingers over mine where I'm clutching the pen and brings my hand to his mouth. I'm shocked to an immobile state as he kisses every knuckle, five times of reverence. It's only when the warmth of his lips fades that I get the function of my body back, enough to pull away my hand, enough to put pen to paper, and start the destruction of a part of my dream.

This is important to me. Was important to me. My hand shakes as I spin the tale, so much that he stills me, tears off the page, and makes me start over.

He kisses my head tenderly, whispering in a soothing tone, "It's all right, little flower. You're doing well."

The untruth burns into my heart as I write it. It's more than lying to my brother. It's admitting that my dream is over, destroyed. That I held out for nothing. That it's never going to happen. No knight is going to charge in on a white horse and save me, just like Damian had said.

So, I do. I write it. I say Maxime's words. At the end, I sign off with, *I love you, always.* It's the only piece of truth in the letter, the part that will tell Damian the rest is false. I never say I love him. I don't have to. He knows. Damian and I don't use that kind of language with each other. Maybe it's because our parents couldn't tell us they loved us, and we've always felt awkward admitting the words.

I turn my face to look up at Maxime. He's shaking his head, giving me a disapproving tsk of his tongue. "That's one of the things I find so endearing about you. It's your will to survive." He strokes a hand over my head. "Just like a little wildflower."

Feigning innocence, I ask, "What do you mean?"

He straightens, takes his phone out of his pocket, swipes over the screen, and turns it to me.

I suck in a breath. On the screen is a copy of a letter, the last one I wrote to Damian. He flicks his finger again. Another letter. Again and again. All my letters.

"Where did you get these?" I cry out.

He tilts his head, giving me time to figure it out for myself.

"Zane da Costa." I say the name like a curse.

"You'll sign it Zoe with two x's and two o's like you always do." He tears off the page, crumples it in his fist, and indicates the blank sheet.

With no choice, I start again, writing Maxime's words but signing as myself.

"That's better," he says, folding the page exactly in the middle and sliding it into one of the matching envelopes with the hotel logo, proof that I've truly left the country, and proof that I'm in a luxurious hotel on my dream vacation.

Oh, my God. That's why Maxime did it. That's why the sly bastard brought me here. It's for appearances sake. If Damian had any doubts after reading my letter, this would convince him I met a wealthy stranger who treats me like a princess. It will smooth over any concerns Damian may have, because princesses are loved and adored.

I twist in the chair to face the man who made me a hostage. Hostages aren't loved and adored. They're used and manipulated. "You're a bastard."

"Shh." He plants a kiss on my head, looking smug as he slips the envelope into the inside pocket of his jacket. "You've been a good girl. Get your coat. It's time for your reward."

I stand on wooden legs. When I don't move for several seconds, Maxime fetches the pink coat and throws it over my shoulders. He hands me a fur-trimmed wool hat and matching scarf. I feel frozen, my fingers too stiff to obey the signals from my brain as he helps me into the coat and buttons it up. He fits the scarf and hat, and finally the gloves, dressing me like a child.

He seems like a happy tourist looking forward to exploring a new city when he pulls on his own coat, scarf, and gloves.

"Have you been here before?" I blurt out, because the guard I should be keeping on my tongue seemed to have shut down with my mental and physical functions.

"Many times," he says.

My tone is biting. "Then this should be very boring for you."

"But it makes me the perfect tour guide." He offers his arm.

I let him hook his arm through mine. I've already fought too many battles with him that I can't win. I need to save my energy for the ones that matter.

Outside the room, Gautier and Benoit stand guard, just like Maxime had said. They nod at Maxime in greeting but ignore me. We go down a hallway with beautiful paintings and mirrors and descend a staircase with a carved wooden rail. The lobby is extravagantly furbished with tones of burgundy and gold. We cross a marble foyer, and then we're in a cobblestone street.

A blast of cold air hits me, making my eyes water. Of course. It's winter here. I didn't think about it, not even when Maxime dressed me up in warm clothes. Abstractly, the knowledge registered, but my brain was on shutdown. The sudden chill makes me shiver.

Maxime pulls me closer. "Warm enough?"

I stiffen. I'm not, but I nod. I walk next to him, deflated, while Gautier and Benoit follow. I absently take in the sights Maxime points out, not to spite him or myself, but because I simply can't gather any enthusiasm, let alone excitement. My mind takes in the beautiful city, but my heart doesn't process the sensory experiences as joy.

We visit Saint Mark's Basilica, Dodge's Palace, and the Rialto Bridge. At each one, we pose for photos Benoit takes with Maxime's phone. I smile when Maxime tells me to, the gesture stiff and unnatural, but when he shows me the photos we look like every other couple in a pose—happy and carefree. It's the trickery of the scenery, of the wind that blows wisps of hair across my face, hiding my expression and making us look breathlessly windblown instead of cruel and trapped. I suppose the photos are more evidence in case my friends back home ask questions. Maybe Maxime will even include one in the letter to Damian.

In the afternoon, we stop for pizza. Maxime says the restaurant is famous throughout the world and that I'll spot some of the Italian *families* dining there. I don't care about spotting infamous mafia members. I eat the pizza and drink the wine, noticing in the back of my mind that the bill is the price of buying a pizza franchise back home. Maxime does all the talking, keeping a steady conversation, but the words float into one ear and out of the other. I'm in a strange kind of limbo. It feels as if I'm not present but staring down at myself from somewhere else, somewhere safer.

"Coffee?" Maxime asks, pulling my attention to him after the waiter has cleared our dessert plates. "Or maybe tea?"

"No, thank you."

"Did you like the tiramisu?"

I look at him. I don't answer, because I really don't know.

His mouth tightens. "Zoe."

"Yes."

He smiles. "Good." Getting up, he holds out a hand. "Come."

Outside, he stops at the flower market to buy a huge bouquet of pink roses. They really are pretty and smell divine. I expect him to take more photos with the flowers as another one of his props, but he seems to be done with the photos. Benoit carries the flowers while Maxime helps me into a gondola. The oarsman speaks to Maxime in Italian. I'm not sure what they say, but Maxime is fluent in the language.

The oarsman steers us down the canal, under bridges and archways, singing passionate songs of love while I sit next to Maxime with a blanket draped over our legs. He's holding my hand as if we are lovers and not as if he has a gun tucked in his waistband under his jacket and his two guards aren't following in their own gondola a short distance behind.

Around the bend, the oarsman stops for us to admire the sunset. It's chilly, and I'm grateful when we finally get off and start making our way back to the hotel. My legs are tired, and I want to crawl into bed and curl into a ball, hiding from *him*, from myself, and most of all from the next four years.

We stop on the square. It's not until Maxime frames my face between his broad palms that I notice Gautier and Benoit have fallen slightly behind, giving us space.

"Zoe." Just from the way my name is a sigh on his lips I know what's to follow is going to be heavy. "Did you have fun today?"

I return from whatever spell I'd been in, my consciousness being thrown back into the moment. Like when he grabbed me in the lobby of my apartment block, my senses become heightened and my awareness sharp. Instinctively, I sense this is important, that the moment has detrimental effects on my wellbeing.

I nod, because I don't want to displease him.

"Good." He smiles, rubbing his thumbs over my cheeks. "Now use your words."

"Yes." Belatedly, I add, "Thank you."

"I want you to listen very carefully to me," he continues. "Remember what I said about choices?"

I nod again, my anxiety mounting.

"I'm going to give you one, maybe the most important one you'll ever make, and I want you to think carefully. I want you to make it wisely. Understand?" He shakes me a little when I don't answer. "Do you understand?"

I don't, but the word he expects slips from my lips. "Yes."

Letting me go, he takes a step back. For a moment, he hesitates, but then he takes my hand and leads me toward an alley. He's walking so fast I have to run to keep up, and by the time we enter a dark, narrow, passageway, he's almost dragging me behind him.

"Maxime." I pull on his hand, trying to get him to slow down, but he won't look at me.

We follow another passageway, this one even narrower, that cuts toward the canal. Under a bridge, we take a staircase that descends to a level below the buildings. The staircase is cold and moldy, the stone walls wet. It leads to a room that seems to be under the water level, maybe an old part of a house before the foundations of the city sank below the sea.

"What is this?" I ask, blinking for my eyes to adjust.

The only light comes from a ventilation hole with an iron grid high up on the wall, just below the ceiling.

Maxime turns to look at me, his eyes flat and emotionless in the dusky interior. He pulls me closer, flush against his body, and folds my arms behind my back. Something clips around my wrists.

"Maxime," I cry out on a whisper.

He slams my back against the wall and takes something from his pocket. I watch in horror as he peels away the backing of a piece of duct tape.

"Maxime! What are you—?"

He seals my lips with the tape, pressing so hard my head knocks against one of the stone bricks. Stars explode behind my eyelids. I shake my head, trying to clear my vision, and when I open my eyes again, I'm just in time to see him fling an iron gate shut, and then a heavy wooden door.

CHAPTER 5

Zoe

Semi-darkness folds around me with the turn of the key. Running to the door, I slam a shoulder against it. The only noises I can get out are panicked mm's. All I get in return is Maxime's retreating footsteps. His heels clack on the stairs, then farther overhead, and finally nothing.

Silence.

I sag against the wall, shaking from head to toe. I can't believe he did this. I can't believe he left me here. Alone. But why is that so hard to believe? He's cruel, not kind.

The shadows are creeping up on me fast. Soon, it will be completely dark. I look around while I can still make out shapes in the dusk. A bench is pushed up against the wall. Other than that, there's nothing.

A sense of abandonment washes over me. I feel lost and alone, but that's nothing compared to the betrayal that burns in my stomach.

Panic.

I have to get out of here. The only hole in this godforsaken place is the ventilation gap, and that's not big enough for a cat to squeeze through, not that I'll ever reach that high, not even standing on the bench.

I go still, taking in the quiet.

Think, Zoe. Think.

It's not completely quiet. The silence I registered after the absence of human voices—Maxime's and my own—is in fact, now that I listen, permeated with the lap of water and the distant hum of a motorboat.

Maybe if I make enough noise someone will hear me. I grab the idea like a life buoy, kicking the walls with the heels and toes of my boots until my feet hurt. When that doesn't work, I kick over the bench and drive it repeatedly into the wall with my feet, but I'm under the water level, and the stone walls must be thick. No one will hear me through the massive door.

The hopelessness of the situation drives me to my knees. I hit the wet, cold, hard floor with my hands handcuffed behind my back, staring up at the hole that goes black as the night sets in.

Despite my coat, hat, scarf, and gloves, I'm cold. I force myself back onto my feet, struggling to do so with my hands tied, but I eventually manage by using the wall as a support. I trace the diameter of the room, turning in circles to create heat and stay warm, but the space is too small for the exercise to work effectively. I jump up and down for as long as I can, but eventually I tire too much.

I turn the bench back over with a foot and sit down. The only way I'm getting out of here is if someone lets me. Maybe nobody will. Maybe that's why Maxime left me here.

To die.

I start crying shamefully as the notion takes form like a living, breathing monster in my chest. A squeaky noise stills me. Something scurries over my hands. Screaming behind the duct tape, I jump up. More squeaking sounds.

Rats.

My teeth start to chatter. I huddle in a corner just like I used to when I was a child. Only, my fairytales can't save me any longer. This is a nightmare, and it's real.

Is Maxime coming back?

He has my letter and the photos. He has my phone. He can send the photos to Damian and my friends, showing them what a great time I'm having. Everyone who knows me even a little knows I've always wanted to come to Venice. Everyone knows I've stupidly been waiting for love to find me, for the right man to save me. Eloping with a stranger is such a *me* thing to do. No one is going to come looking for me. I'll vanish off the face of the earth. My bones will rot in this burial chamber under the canals of Venice, the city of my dreams.

I can't help but laugh hysterically through my tears. What a stupid idiot I've been. So naïve.

Sniffing, I wipe my cheek on my shoulder. Feeling sorry for myself isn't going to help. It's not the fear of dying that hits me hardest in the gut. It's the regret. It's not paying closer attention when Maxime said it wouldn't always be like this. His meaning was obvious, yet my mind rejected it, choosing not to see it. It's not heeding Maxime's words when he told me to make the best of the day, most probably the last day of my life.

CHAPTER 6

Maxime

Back at the hotel, I dismiss my guards and have a long, warm shower. Then I order room service, put on a classical music collection, and arrange the roses in the vase while I wait for my food to be delivered.

It arrives promptly, a steak the way I like—rare—with garlic and parsley potatoes on the side and a bottle of their best red. The cutlery is silver and the glass crystal. The candle on the table is scented. It smells of lavender. Tomorrow, I'll ask them to get some rose-scented ones.

I eat everything, enjoying the warmth of my suite and the view over the square. When I'm done, I pour four fingers of cognac from the wet bar and walk to the window to stare at the canal. It's pretty at night with lanterns hanging over the bridges. So romantic. Such an illusion. Under the beautiful streets where tourists eat, laugh, and shop, lies my buried treasure. Somewhere down there under the dirty water is a little flower, a yellow daisy that will wilt and die without sunlight or water.

I stopped smoking years ago, but I wrap my coat around my body and take the packet I nicked from Gautier out onto the balcony. Lighting one up, I drag the smoke into my lungs. If she's suffering, so will I. It's the least I can give her. Stripping naked, I bare my body to the cold. As always, the freezing pain settling in my toes and fingers grounds me.

I don't finish the cigarette.

I put it out on my chest.

CHAPTER 7

Zoe

When I doze off, the rats soon discover I'm a harmless target and nip at the exposed flesh of my wrists and even at my legs through my tights. I swat and kick at them, but they're becoming fearless, even taking their chances when I'm awake. The broken skin burns at first, but after a while the cold numbs everything, so much so I don't feel the bite of pain as their sharp teeth gnaw at my flesh. The best way of warding them off is moving, but they follow and try to climb up my legs when they can't bite through my boots.

By the time the sun comes up, I'm exhausted and cold to my core. It's as if the damp has infiltrated my bones. I can't stand on my feet anymore. I think the rats may kill me before I starve. I'm not sure which is the most merciful. My stockings are torn and the expensive clothes ruined, dirty from the damp and black mold on the walls. It stinks worse than my apartment building down here.

Leaning against the wall, I kick at a rat that climbs onto the toe of my boot. The slosh of the water is quieter. It's low tide. There's something else, too, like the fall of a hammer. It comes closer. No, it's the fall of footsteps. My heart starts thundering in my chest when they descend down the steps. I brace myself, praying for rescue, but the door swings open on Maxime's face.

He's wearing a pale suit with a pink tie, and his face is clean-shaven. When he opens the gate and enters my prison, a whiff of winter reaches my nostrils. It's clean and fresh, a stark contrast to my dirt and exhaustion, like a magnifying glass on his cruelty. He's cold and monstrous.

He's not my savior.

I back away, but he grips my hair with one hand, and carefully pulls off the tape with the other. It hurts. The skin on my lips stretches and cracks. I drag my tongue over them and taste blood.

Something inside me snaps. My vision turns blurry.

He turns me around to undo the cuffs. The moment my hands are free, I jump at him. I claw and hit, screaming like a mad person. I must be mad, because what I should be doing is escaping. I kick. I punch him in the gut. He only stands there and takes it, my blows doing no damage. After the next fist I jam into his stomach, I shove him and run.

I'm not even on the first step before he grabs hold of my ankle. I go down, stopping my fall with my hands. The heels of my palms burn as the skin comes off, but I kick with all my might. I dig my fingers into the stone, my nails breaking as he drags me back into my cell.

"No!"

He flips me onto my back and covers my mouth with his hand. My lips are pulled back, my jaw wide. I bite down until the pressure of his hand becomes so severe, I think my skull may crack.

"Are you done?" he asks through thin lips.

I shake my head, but we both know I am. The fight goes out of me, my energy spent.

"If you scream," he says, "I'll leave. I can do this for days until you're ready to listen."

When I go still, he removes his hand. "That's better."

I lie on my back on the damp stones, the wetness seeping through my coat and dress, through my very skin and into my heart. He's crouching next to me, studying me with one arm braced on his knee. His frame is big and powerful. The shadow he casts over me swallows me whole. Somehow, it seems darker and colder than the winter night I spent in my cell.

"I want you to listen to me, Zoe."

My gaze homes in on his face, on the non-symmetrical lines of his features and the bump on the bridge of his nose.

"When I take you home," he continues in his musical accent, "you have a choice."

My hope lifts a fraction. "To South Africa?"

"To France."

The words are a punch. I don't know how many more punches I can take. I force the question from numb lips. "What choice?"

"It can be like yesterday, like the day we spent, or it can be like this." He motions around the space. "What you decide is entirely up to you, but you should know that each choice comes with a price."

I hold my breath, waiting for him to carry on.

"If I take you to my family in France, this is what awaits you. You'll be locked up, a prisoner. The men will take turns with you, starting with my brother, and he's not a kind man. He'll keep you alive, but you'll wish you were dead. The only way I can protect you is to lay claim to you." His gaze pierces mine. "Do you understand what I'm saying?"

My body is shaking uncontrollably, my mind refusing to give meaning to the words.

"Do you understand, Zoe?"

I shake my head.

"You're going to have to become my mistress." The flames in his eyes burn glacially. "You're going to have to let me fuck you, convincingly and often."

CHAPTER 8

Maxime

Zoe's pretty, blue eyes flare, as always giving away her heart. She finds the idea of me fucking her disgusting. I didn't expect otherwise. Nonetheless, it stabs into my chest.

I bet she'll find Alexis handsome. All the women do, until they discover his fetishes.

She licks her cracked lips. "Are you asking me to sell my body in exchange for your protection?"

"I don't need to buy sex, little flower." Despite my physique, I have enough eager bed partners.

"You mean your mistress as for real?"

I nod, a sadistic part of me enjoying her discomfort for making her distaste so obvious. "For real."

I can almost see her brain kicking back into action. "Why can't we pretend? Why do I have to sleep with you?"

"Because my family will know." More accurately, my father and brother.

"How?"

"Believe me, there are signs that will be obvious." I fuck hard. My family knows me. My lovers don't walk straight in the morning, not that they're complaining. There will be medical checkups, birth control, and our doctor is a family friend. He'll report back to my father. Changing to a different practitioner will be suspicious, a dead giveaway. No, there's only one way of playing this.

For real.

She swallows. "Why would you help me?"

Yes, why indeed? "Because I'd hate to see your life wasted."

She blinks, her lashes wet with unshed tears. "Isn't it already wasted?"

"Choice, Zoe. It all depends on how you choose to look at it."

Sniffing, she turns her face to the light that falls in a wedge from the hole in the wall. Between the two options, I know, and she knows what her choice is going to be. I let her have the moment, let her bask in denial for a little while longer.

When she finally looks back at me, her tears are spilling over. It both pains and pleases me how little she wants me and that she's already admitting her defeat, because when she opens her pretty, little mouth, she's going to give me her consent.

She nods, a small movement that barely tilts her head.

I wipe a strand of hair from her dirty face. "Say it." The quicker she consents, the quicker I can carry her out of here, clean her, and give her sunlight and water so she'll flourish again.

"Yes," she says in a faint voice.

"Yes, what?"

"I'll be your mistress."

"That's a good choice, Zoe." I drag my palm over her cheek. "You made it wisely."

I don't waste time. I scoop her up from the cold floor, cradling her against my chest. The demonstration was a hard one, but it was necessary. It hurt me as much as it hurt her. The fresh cigarette burns on my stomach and chest are proof of that.

She weighs nothing in my arms as I mount the stairs. I hold her tighter, sheltering her against the cold as much as I can. She's mine now. I'll take care of her every need.

Gautier waits at the street level with a blanket. He drapes it over her, careful not to touch her, and I tuck it around her body. She's shivering like a petal caught in a storm. We don't go down the alley but take the steps to the jetty where the motorboat is tied. Benoit is aboard. At our approach, he unties the boat. I lower Zoe to her feet and help her inside. When we're all in, I sit, drawing her into my lap and making sure she's covered with the blanket.

Benoit starts the engine and turns the boat into the canal. The wind nips at my face and ears. In the fight, Zoe lost her hat. She draws deeper under the blanket, huddling close to me. It feeds a hungry part of me. I open my jacket and pull it around her under the blanket so the heat from my body can warm her better.

After a short ride, we moor the boat in front of our hotel. It's early. Few people are about. I lift Zoe out and carry her inside while my men scout the area ahead of us. We don't run into anyone in the lobby or on the stairs, and a few minutes later we're back in the suite.

Carrying her straight to the bathroom, I lower her onto the bench next to the bath before crouching in front of her. When I reach for the blanket, she clutches it tighter to her chest.

"What are you doing?" she asks.

"You need a shower." When the pleat on her brow doesn't smooth out, I explain my intention. "I'm not going to hurt you. I need to take care of you."

"Then get out."

I stand. The rejection stings, but I welcome the hurt. Feeling something after nothing, after thinking I'd never feel again, is a miracle and joyful in itself.

She agreed. I want to remind her, but I have to be patient. In fact, it's better I don't see her naked before tonight. The drawn-out expectation will only heighten the pleasure.

Still, I'm not comfortable leaving her in this state. She's tired and weak. She can slip in the shower and crack open her head.

"Please?" she says.

The word pulls at my heart, another foreign sensation, because I do want to please her.

"Call if you need me." I turn and leave but stop in the door. "Maybe it's better if you have a bath."

"I'll be fine," she says, her eyes sparking with annoyance.

I smile in return. "I'm right outside."

Her rosebud mouth turns down. "Isn't that good to know?"

I let it slide. I'm so happy to have her consent.

Closing the door to give her privacy, I settle down at the bureau in the bedroom so I can hear her in case she changes her mind about needing my help. I summon Benoit and give him the letter to mail with an instruction to bring back a tetanus shot. We have contacts everywhere. I can get anything I want, no matter where I am.

The water in the shower comes on. By the time it turns off, I've ordered brunch and made arrangements for tonight. When Zoe steps out dressed in a bathrobe, I point at the loveseat.

She trots over, but falters before she reaches the seat. "Are you going to do it now?"

My grin is diabolic. I know what she means, but I want her to say it. "Do what?"

"You know." She waves at the bed.

"You mean fuck you?"

Her cheeks turn a deep pink, pretty like a fuchsia rose.

I watch her with my hands folded behind my back, enjoying her shyness. "We don't need a bed to fuck. We can do it on other furniture, in many different places, and in a variety of positions." But for our first time, it will be in the bed.

She swallows. "I'm not ready."

What does she need to be ready? Definitely not clothes. I enjoy playing this game of cat and mouse with her, but I want her relaxed, not stressed. I want her to enjoy it. It's in both our interest that I put her mind at ease.

"Don't worry." I walk closer. "You have time."

Her shoulders sag. Does she know how openly she shows her relief? "Until when?"

"Tonight."

Nighttime is when lovers do it, at least the first time. Or so I presume. I've never been the romantic type. I've never been anyone's lover. I've fucked enough times to have refined the technique of giving a woman pleasure to an art, but I've never been with the same woman more than a couple of times. I'm actually looking forward to exploring long-term sex with Zoe, which is why the first time is important. The first time of everything determines how the rest of it will go.

Taking her hand, I pull her down onto the seat. Then I crouch in front of her and brush the robe away to expose her legs. She sits quietly, albeit tensely, as I inspect the bite marks on her legs. I push back the sleeves and turn her wrists this way and that to do the same. Finally, I straighten to drag my fingers through her hair and over her scalp, feeling for bumps. There's a small one at the back of her head.

"Do you have pain?" I ask.

She shakes her head.

"Are you hungry?"

"Thirsty," she says.

"I'll feed you soon."

I leave her on the loveseat to take the medicine kit from my bag. I never travel without one. It's a must in our business. Meticulously, I disinfect every mark and scratch on her skin, including the heels of her palms.

The brunch arrives just as I've finished. I don't make her sit at the table but order her to bed and fluff out the pillows behind her back. I serve a savory muffin, bacon, and scrambled eggs onto a plate and let her eat in bed while I pour rose petal tea into a cup to cool.

Benoit returns with the tetanus vaccine as I carry her empty plate away. I first give her an anti-inflammatory pill to drink with her tea, and then I take a hypodermic syringe from the kit.

Her eyes widen when I insert the needle into the vial. "What are you doing?"

"It's a tetanus shot," I explain, "for the bites."

She says nothing as I push the sleeve of the robe up and lock my fingers around her arm. She flinches when I insert the needle into her skin and empty the syringe, but she's a brave girl. She doesn't complain.

With my charge taken care of, I'm a lot happier, certainly less miserable than last night. The only thing left is for her to get some rest.

Stroking her soft hair that's still damp after her shower, I say, "Close your eyes. Sleep. You must be tired."

She doesn't argue. Her long lashes flutter over her eyes, and her face muscles go slack as she eases down onto the mattress. With an unusually docile acceptance, she allows me to pet her hair.

Someday, she'll long for me to touch her like this. There will come a day she won't have to simply tolerate my touch.

When I'm done with her, she's going to need it like a drug.

CHAPTER 9

Zoe

It's dusk when I wake up. The room is basked in a soft, rose-gold glow. I feel a lot better than this morning. My belly is full, my aches are gone, I'm warm, and I'm fully rested. Then a ball of trepidation tightens my stomach, spoiling my good physical state.

In an hour, it will be dark. Sinful things happen in the dark. Prey is hunted and monsters thrive, but vows must be honored, no matter if dreams are destroyed.

I swing my legs over the bed and look around. Thankfully, I'm alone in the room. Not knowing how much I'll be granted in the future, I make the most of the privacy by going to the bathroom to use the facilities, but when I open the door, I'm met with shimmering candlelight and the sensual smell of roses. The tub is filled with steaming water, rose petals drifting on top. Candles burn on the vanity, floor, and edge of the bath. Petals are scattered around them. The scene is so pretty I forget to be angry and even to be anxious for a moment, but then I remember who's set it all up, and my shoulders snap tight with tension again.

I glance back at the room, expecting *him* to be standing there, gauging my reaction, but I'm still alone. The fragrance and the warm water are too enticing to waste. I lock the door and let the robe slip from my shoulders. Tying my hair in a bun on top of my head, I climb into the tub and lower myself into the water.

It's heaven. The warmth seeps into my skin, melting the tightness in my muscles. A flute with bubbly, golden liquid stands within my hand's reach on the windowsill. It's a beautiful glass with intricate engraving. I bring it to my lips and take a sip. The champagne is dry and yeasty. I've had a couple of glasses in my lifetime, at year-end work parties on both occasions, and instantly loved the taste. It's a luxury I could never afford on my grocery budget.

It takes a bit of playing with the settings before I figure out how to make the bubbles work. A stream of water massages my lower back and another my feet. I lay back—there's even a bath pillow for my head—and admire the view of the canal and the bridge below. Lights are twinkling on the bridge, and the streetlamps illuminating the cobblestone street look antique, like something straight from a fairytale. Except, this isn't a fairytale, and I shouldn't forget it.

As reality wiggles back into my consciousness, wiping away the beauty of the moment, I down the champagne in one go. I no longer want to sip it for enjoyment. I only want to use it to dull my senses.

I do have a little buzz when I get out a long while later and dry myself. My thoughts run ahead to what will follow, but they're interrupted by what I find when I walk back into the room. The bed has been freshly made with clean linen. A pink dress is arranged at the foot end. It's the most beautiful creation I've seen. Unable to help myself, I step closer.

It's a long, off-shoulder evening dress. The cut is simple. What makes it extraordinary is the diamante tulle. It's shimmery, delicate, and so faintly pink the color is a mere blush. I love it. It's completely me. The thought makes me go rigid. Of course, Maxime knows. He probably went through my books and sketches when he went back to see Bruce and wipe away the evidence of my existence.

Pink silk underwear and thigh-high stockings with a lace trimming are set out next to the dress. A velvet box catches my eyes. My curiosity piqued, I reach for the box and flip back the lid. A pair of solitaire diamonds sits on a black velvet cushion, their light brighter than sunrays or a rainbow. They're enormous, at least a couple carats. I've never owned a diamond, but I know a lot about them from the clippings I collected of my dream ring, the one the man who loved me was going to offer me.

I close the lid and throw the box back onto the bed.

What am I doing?

How can I admire objects my kidnapper bought? Soon to be my lover. A chill breaks out over my body. When I think of the alternative, of what Maxime showed and told me, I drop the towel and pull on the clothes.

Everything fits perfectly, even the heels that are the same color as the dress. I'm about to go to the bathroom to brush my hair when I notice the silver brush and cosmetics on the bedroom dresser. I go over and trace the embossed rose on the back of the brush. It's beautiful, a piece of art. After removing the elastic keeping up my bun, I pull the brush through my hair, almost closing my eyes at how the soft bristles massage my scalp.

I sit down and look at my reflection in the mirror. I'm pale. I don't want to look pretty for Maxime. I don't want to give him me. Tonight, when I give him my virginity, I want to be someone else, someone I don't care about so I can still face the real me in the mirror tomorrow.

I inspect the makeup. It's an expensive French brand. Other than mascara and lip gloss, I usually don't wear makeup and not because I don't like it. I can't afford it. Now I go for a dramatic look, using smoky eye shadow and black eyeliner that I round off with a pale lipstick. Definitely not me. The sparkling earrings add the finishing touch.

A clutch bag covered with the same cloth as the dress and an intricately sewn rose fastened to the clip stands next to a bottle of perfume. I dab a drop on my wrist to smell it and notice the marks from last night's ordeal. My breathing turns shallow, but I inhale deeply and blow the breath out slowly. I can do this. I can put up this act.

Standing, I regard my image in the mirror. I don't recognize the woman staring back at me. Good.

A knock sounds on the door. When I answer it, Maxime stands on the threshold with a bouquet of flowers. He's dressed in a tux and bowtie, and his hair is damp.

"You showered," I say stupidly, wondering if he's renting another suite.

"I showered in Gautier and Benoit's room. I wanted to give you privacy." His gaze trails over me and fixes on my face. "You look beautiful, Zoe." He holds the flowers out to me. "These are for you."

I take them uncertainly. I don't understand this man who'll lock me up in a dungeon and buy me flowers before stealing what's left of my dream. He doesn't need to woo me. It's not as if we're dating.

"Don't you like them?" he asks.

I look at the cellophane-wrapped bouquet. It's a colorful collection of sweet peas, poppies, daisies, and cornflowers. The arrangement is informal and uninhibited, just like the wildflowers. It's lovely.

"Thank you."

"You'll want to put them in water before we go."

I scoot around him, pulling in my stomach to avoid touching him when he doesn't move out of the way. He watches me as I find a vase on the table and carry it back to the bathroom to fill it with water.

While I take care of the flowers, he blows out the candles, presumably so the suite doesn't burn down while we're out to wherever he's taking me.

"Your bag," he says when I turn to go.

For lipstick, tissues, and powder, and whatever else a woman on a fuck date may need. He really thought about everything. I drop the tube of lipstick and compressed powder inside for the sake of placating him and hold my head high as I walk to the door.

He stands aside for me to exit ahead of him. In the lounge, he drapes a long white coat around my shoulders and hands me a faux-fur scarf.

"Where are we going?" I ask when he offers me his arm.

He smiles down at me. "You'll see."

If this is supposed to be a surprise, it's not the good kind.

Outside, a boat waits. The air is wet and cold. He takes my hand and helps me inside. As before, he sits next to me in the back while Gautier steers and Benoit sits up front.

I stare at the buildings as we pass, trying not to fidget. After a short drive, we stop in front of a building I recognize from my travel books —the Teatro La Fenice. I've read about it extensively. Is this why he brought me here? Because he saw various books about the landmark building in my apartment? I've always wanted to see an opera, just not with Maxime.

The façade is the only part of the opera house that survived the two fires that almost destroyed the building in 1836 and 1996. It's stunning. It bears the theater's insignia in the center, a phoenix rising from the flames. Two statues in niches represent the muses of tragedy and dance. Above them are the masks of Comedy and Tragedy.

The opulence inside is overwhelming. The photos I've seen don't do it justice. I can't help but stare at the golden pillars and detailed ceiling paintings. Maxime steers me to the Royal Box, the best seats in the house. We're barely seated before the first curtain call sounds.

I gasp when the curtains rise to reveal the set of a scene in Egypt. The life-size sphinx and pyramid look so real I'm transported to a different place and time. When the opera starts, I forget about Maxime for a moment. It's Nabucco, goosebumps-worthy and incredibly sad. I loathe to admit I love every minute. When I dare to turn my head in Maxime's direction, I catch him watching me with undisguised fascination, as if my reaction is the real attraction. It makes me feel like a monkey in a zoo.

During intermission, he gets me a glass of freshly squeezed lemon juice with mint. I eye the glass of wine he sips. I could do with more alcohol courage. Too soon, the beautiful performance comes to an end.

Gautier and Benoit stand guard at the entrance to our box when we exit. Maxime says something to Gautier in French, who nods and leaves. Benoit stays behind, following in our footsteps.

"Do you always have protection?" I ask.

Maxime places his hand on the small of my back to steer me down the stairs. "Yes."

"Why? Because your family is involved in criminal activities?"

He glances around and says in a lowered voice, "Because we're powerful."

"That makes you a target?"

"Always." He brushes his thumb over a vertebra. "You have to fight to get to the top, and then you have to fight twice as hard to stay there. There's always someone eager to take your place."

His touch makes me shiver. "Does being at the top matter so much?"

"Yes." His voice is filled with conviction. "In this world, only the strongest survive."

I want to say it's a cynical outlook, but we've arrived at the cloakroom. He gets my coat and makes sure I'm covered before leading me to the boat. His attention is unsettling. He's behaving like the perfect gentleman, but I know who he truly is.

I expect us to go back to the hotel, but Gautier pulls up in front of a small but cozy-looking restaurant. Surely, we're overdressed. When I mention it to Maxime, he only laughs.

Once inside, I understand why Maxime wasn't fazed. We're the only customers. A man in his late fifties pushes through a swing door to greet us. I get a glimpse of the kitchen through the open door. Meat is sizzling on a grill and something is bubbling in a pot. An aroma of oregano and garlic fills the air.

"Max." The man slaps him on the back and says something in Italian.

Maxime replies, after which the man addresses me in English. "Welcome to my humble restaurant. I will do my best to satisfy your appetite. I'm Matteo, but you can call me Teo."

I smile stiffly, my nerves getting the better of me. "Thank you."

Teo leads us to a small veranda where a table with a crisp white tablecloth is set with crystal and silverware. The terrace is encased in glass, keeping the cold out while allowing a view over the canal. A creeper grows over the trellis, and glass balls with tea candles dangle at different heights from the ceiling. It's breathtaking. With the moon hanging low over the water between the buildings, it's picture perfect.

Teo seats us, then bustles off and returns with olive bread and tapenade.

"I thought you'd be more at ease with an informal setting tonight," Maxime says when Teo is gone.

I glance at the empty tables. "You booked out the whole place?"

"It's more intimate, no?"

Intimate isn't where I want to go. When I toy with the stem of my glass, Maxime asks, "Thirsty?"

I nod.

He serves sparkling water for me and wine for himself.

"Is there a reason I'm not allowed to drink wine?" I ask.

"A good one."

"That is?"

His eyes darken. "I want you lucid tonight."

My stomach flips. He wants me to remember our first time.

Teo saves me from a response by arriving with a selection of small dishes.

"I thought we'd just nibble," Maxime says, "as you may be too nervous for a heavy meal."

His seductive accent chills me to the bone. His insight sets me further on edge. I don't want him to know what I think or feel. Especially, not what I feel.

He leans closer, his gaze sharp and predatory. "I can make it very good for you, Zoe. All you have to do is relax. I'll take care of everything."

My cheeks heat, as Teo is still busy shifting the dishes around to fit everything on the table.

When Teo is gone again, Maxime drops the lustful tone and talks about the opera while he serves me. Like the night he took me to

Seven Seas, he proves how skillful he is at the art of making conversation, keeping it light while the stone in my stomach is heavy and I don't have words.

If not for the circumstances, the evening might've been pleasant, but I can't wait for it to be over. I'm half relieved and half terrified when Maxime finally stands and offers me a hand.

His gray stare is as intense as his words are charged. "Shall we go?"

Clearing my throat, I push back my chair. I consider not taking his hand, but after a moment's hesitation I accept. This is one of those battles not worth fighting.

The closer we get to the hotel, the tighter my stomach grows. I think I may be sick. I hate him, even if he's saving me from a worse fate. If he hadn't taken me to start with, I wouldn't have been in this awful position.

I glance at his face from under my lashes as Gautier drives. The man I'm about to accept as my lover is harsh, unfeeling, unattractive, and a kidnapper. I don't understand why he went to so much trouble for me tonight. I do, however, believe he does nothing without purpose, and that makes me question his motives. He doesn't need to give me consideration, attention, or lavish treatment.

He turns his head a fraction, catching me staring. "Don't like what you see?"

Unable to admit the truth, I avert my eyes.

His easy acceptance of the unspoken insult tells me that one, he gets that a lot, and two, it doesn't faze him.

By the time we're back at the hotel, I'm a wreck. I climb the stairs ahead of the men, my back stiff and chin high. Maxime bids the guards good night on the landing and opens the door for me.

Once inside, my bravado falters. I stop in the lounge. What now? How is this supposed to happen? Do I go to the room and get naked? Wait for him in the bed? At the thought, a shiver crawls over my skin.

In no hurry, Maxime removes his jacket and drapes it over the clotheshorse. He undoes his tie and pours himself a whiskey from the wet bar. Sipping it, he studies me quietly. Unlike me, he doesn't seem uncertain. It looks as if he knows exactly what he's going to do next.

I have an urge to wring my hands together. Instead, I force them behind my back. I'm not giving him the satisfaction of knowing he'll be my first. I lock that knowledge away, hanging onto it selfishly for as long as I can. He doesn't deserve it. Hopefully, he won't even notice.

"Zoe."

I jump at the sound of his voice, giving away my anxiety. The timbre is deep and velvety, the way he says my name in his foreign accent like a caress. I barely suppress the rebellious instinct to defy him.

"Do you need to use the bathroom?" he asks.

Not trusting my voice, I shake my head.

He says in a low voice, "Then go to the room, *cherie*."

CHAPTER 10

Zoe

The words are like a sentence, the lash of a whip on my back. A sense of pending loss hangs over me, but I squash it and lock down my emotions as I do what he says and go to the room. I throw the clutch onto the loveseat where he treated my wounds this morning and stop next to the bed. When he enters the room, courage hangs around me like a shroud.

I square my shoulders, my false bravado back in place. "How do you want me?"

He tilts his head and studies me curiously. "How do you mean?"

I curl my fingers until my nails cut into my palms. "Naked or clothed?"

A slow smile curves his lips. "I don't fuck a woman with her clothes on."

"Naked, then," I say with a bite in my tone. "On the bed? Bent over the dresser?"

"Zoe." He shakes his head, amusement making the flat gray of his eyes seems livelier, like quicksilver. "Slow down."

"Just do it already." I only want this to be over.

He walks to me slowly, working his bowtie free. "Fucking isn't only about me driving my dick into your pussy."

My cheeks heat at his crass language. When he hands me his tumbler, I take it in a reflex reaction. He unbuttons his collar before taking back the glass and leaving it on the dresser. His actions are fluid, self-assured. He stares deep into my eyes, penetrating every corner of the parts I try to hide from him as he cups my face between his broad palms.

His skin is warm and calloused on my cheeks. I gasp as he tilts my head back and lowers his with slow purpose. I know he's going to kiss me, but nothing prepares me for the moment his lips touch mine.

I expected to be repulsed, as I expected him to strip me naked and use me. I didn't expect him to kiss me and certainly not like this. It's tentative, exploring. His lips are warm and soft, and the gentle pressure on mine wakes the nerve endings under my skin. When he releases my lips, I stare up at his face with a mixture of surprise and confusion.

"What are you doing?" I manage on a whisper.

He scans my face, studying my eyes before his gaze drops to my lips. Instead of answering, he presses our mouths together again. This time there's a crackle of a spark where his lips brush over mine. I gasp, a soft intake of breath. His eyes darken at the sound. The lust burns brightly in his, but before apprehension can take root, he deepens the kiss.

The only parts of our bodies touching are his hands on my cheeks and our lips, but it's already a sensory overload. His clean smell infiltrates my nose—citrus and spices. The warmth of his hands seeps into my skin. I'm unprepared, and the new sensations catch me off-guard. Maybe I wouldn't have been so susceptible if this wasn't my first kiss. I can only blame myself for holding out for a futile fantasy. I can only blame my inexperience for being so utterly defenseless against his skillful lips.

Goosebumps break out over my arms when he sucks my bottom lip into his mouth. He nips the flesh softly with his teeth and then lets go to plant a butterfly kiss on the same spot. Heat surges through my veins, my body reacting violently to the light stimulation. When he traces the seam of my lips with his tongue, my lips open of their own accord. He steals inside, intensifying the kiss further. He tastes of whiskey and man. The gentle way he molds his lips over mine weakens my knees. My body starts to hum, electricity tingling under my overly sensitive skin. All the while, he holds me carefully, framing my face like I'm a fragile doll.

My breathing spikes. My breasts tighten. An ache starts to pulse between my legs. A moan escapes my lips, bursting like a bubble in our kiss. Need rises in my body as the kiss becomes more demanding. I answer it without thinking, tangling my tongue with his. The minute I return the caress with equal measure, he walks me backward until my body collides with the window. The curtains haven't been drawn. The pane is cold on my back, emphasizing how overheated my skin is.

He leans in, pressing his body against mine. There's something about being held like this by a man. I can't put my finger on it, only that it makes me want to submit to his possession, to be dominated by his strength and protected by his power. I fall effortlessly into the trap. My lifelong tendency to escape via dreaming is a well-practiced skill. It easily aids my mind away from reality to the fantasy that's played off so many times in my dreams that I'm longing for it with constant desire.

He's hard and solid, a wall of muscle. His erection presses against my stomach, feeding me my own measure of power. Male power has always featured in my fantasies about sex, but I never knew I'd have some of my own. It's liberating, soothing my resentment of our unequal standing. The small part of my mind that still functions processes and stores the new knowledge. The only place I'll ever have power is in his bed.

His hands leave my face to slide down my neck and over my shoulders. They roam over my arms and come to rest on my hips. Through it all, he doesn't break the kiss. Our life forces are mingled, the air we inhale the same. My breathing becomes more labored as Maxime lays a palm over my stomach. I know he can feel the rapid movement of my in- and exhales, my need for more. It's as if he does just that, measures my reaction, before moving his hand to the underside of my breast. I gasp, my body going still in anticipation. Cautiously, he drags his hand higher until his thumb brushes my nipple. When the tip hardens under his touch, a growl escapes his chest.

Our kiss turns frantic, my fantasy urgent and his victory a foregone conclusion. I can't describe what his hands on me feel like. I've never experienced such crazed need. I don't even know what to expect, only that it's natural when he bunches the dress in a fist and pulls it up to my hip so his free hand can slip underneath and cup the heat between my legs.

My moan is mindless, shameful. My underwear is wet. The sound he makes when he discovers this is closer to animal than man. Abandoning the private place no man has ever touched, he grips the zipper on the side of the dress. It makes a scratchy sound as he pulls it down. He's gentle as he slips the sleeve off my shoulder. The fabric pools around my waist. He holds my gaze as he pushes it over my hips, letting the dress fall around my feet. The gray of his eyes is smoky, the usual coldness burning hot. I'm mesmerized by their transformation, staring at the way the color darkens to molten mercury as he takes a step back and drags his gaze over me.

The distance leaves me cold. It breaks the feverish spell. It shocks me back to the moment, dousing my desire with shame. I flatten by back against the glass, trying to put distance between us, but Maxime scoops me up in his arms and carries me to the bed. He lowers me carefully to the mattress, leaving my legs dangling over the edge. When he crouches down, I push up on my elbows with anxious expectation, but he only reaches for my foot. He takes off first the one, then the other shoe, kissing the bridge of each foot. Then he straightens again and grips the elastic of my thigh-high stocking. I watch as he rolls it down and discards it before doing the same with the other. It's when he reaches for the panties that I stiffen.

"Shh." He leans over me, kisses my lips, and pushes me back with a palm on my chest until my arms give out and my back hits the mattress. "Just relax."

I don't. I pinch my eyes shut as he pulls the underwear over my hips and feet. I feel him move over me and jerk when he places a kiss at the top of my sex.

"Look at me, Zoe."

Reluctantly, I open my eyes.

"That's better," he says. "I want to see your expression when I make you come."

When he reaches for the bra, I automatically put a hand over his to still him.

He doesn't force it. Instead, he says, "Take off your bra for me. I want to see all of you."

I'm already naked from the waist down, but I hesitate. Somehow, I'm reluctant to remove this last barrier. He waits patiently. He's not going anywhere until I comply. Refusing is only pulling this out longer.

My hands shake slightly as I unclip the front clasp.

"Take it off completely," he says.

I push the straps from my shoulders, pulling one arm free at a time.

He does a slow evaluation of my body. "You're beautiful, my little flower. Gorgeous, just like I knew you'd be."

He pushes to his feet and unbuckles his belt. He lets it hangs loose as he removes his shoes and socks, and then the pants. He watches me intently as he pushes his briefs over his hips, so much so that I can't look at him and have to turn my head to the side.

"Eyes on me, Zoe."

The stern command is in stark contrast to the gentleness of earlier. Slowly, I face him again as he opens two buttons of his shirt from the bottom up. The shirttails don't hide his hardness. His cock is thick and long, jutting out proudly. He's huge. The sight is more erotic than I expected, making my lower body heat. I've never seen a man so close to naked or a stiff cock peeking out from the folds of his shirt front.

I try to scoot back when he steps between my legs, but he grabs my thighs and spreads them wide before going down on his knees.

"What are you doing?" I cry out.

His lips quirk in one corner. "What does it look like?"

He lowers his head, watching me watching him as he presses a kiss right in the center of my legs. My whole body jerks.

He gives me a knowing smile. "No one has ever gone down on you?"

I want to say yes, to tell a lie, but the sweep of his tongue over my folds steals my words. It's hot. It's delicious. Grabbing my knees, he keeps my legs open and licks from the bottom to the top of my slit. My thighs quake. The swipe of his tongue over my clit makes my back arch.

"So responsive," he says, sounding pleased.

When he sucks lightly on the bundle of nerves, my body bows. The pleasure is exquisite. Heat unfurls and coils in my lower body, spinning a web of need. It climbs, transporting me to a place I desperately need to go, but then he slows down. I fist my hands in the sheets in frustration. Devouring me, he keeps his gaze on my face, gauging my reaction. He uses his thumbs to spread me, then nips and licks until the tightly coiled tension is about to snap, but just before it does, he slows down again.

I moan in frustration. "Maxime."

His tone is lazy, teasing almost. "What is it, *ma belle*?"

"Please." Make it stop.

"Do you want to come?"

No, not like this but being kept on the edge of something unknown is torture.

"You have to say it," he says.

Even in this, he forces my consent. Yet just like with our warped arrangement, he doesn't give me a choice. Not really. Not when he's tormenting me with his erotic administrations.

The word escapes on a defeated breath from my lips. "Yes."

He immediately complies, focusing all his wicked attention on my clit. He drags his tongue in circles and bites down gently before flicking the tip of his tongue over the flesh that feels engorged and needy.

At last, the tension snaps. Fireworks set off in my core. My muscles contract, my legs hugging his face as he continues his assault and pushes me higher, still. It's better and worse than I imagined. Better because the pleasure is unique, a powerful sensation unlike any other. Worse, because the surrender tastes like defeat. The relief is physical. The agony is mental.

The thoughts lash at me as I lie naked and spread with my ecstasy on display, little shocks tightening my sex while Maxime studies me, studies his work. I wish I could disappear within myself like yesterday when he forced me to write the letter, but the pleasure grounds me. I'm fully present in the moment.

As Maxime shifts me to the middle of the bed and stretches out over me, I tell myself I'm someone else, the woman with the dark makeup. When he aligns his cock with my entrance, I don't want to feel the heat that liquefies my center. I want to be cold and frigid, but I'm aroused and on fire.

He threads his fingers through my hair, holding my head gently as he stares into my eyes. The moment imprints in my memory. What we're about to do, neither of us can ever erase. It's nothing, just sex, and yet it's everything. It's my whole life's worth of dreaming combined. Destroyed. When the head of his cock nudges my folds apart and my wetness coats him, I see the pleasure in his eyes. I hope he can see the hate in mine. I hate him, but not nearly as much as I hate myself for what he makes me feel.

When he pushes forward, parting me, I grab his upper arms despite my intention not to touch him. It burns. It feels like he'll split me in two.

"Shh." He kisses my forehead. "You'll adapt in a minute."

I don't, but he's patient. He moves slowly. When he slides another inch inside, I start to panic. He's too big. It hurts too much.

"It'll soon be better," he says.

His promise is a lie, because the more he stretches me the more it hurts. He seems to have difficulty entering me deeper. My breath catches. I clench my teeth, trying not to show him my agony.

Bringing his hands to my face, he brushes his thumbs over my cheeks. "You're tight, my little flower." His voice is strained. "Has it been a while?"

I can't speak for the fear of giving myself away. I don't deny or admit it. I only focus on breathing through the intrusion that burns like fire and makes me regret not choosing a cell full of rats over this.

He pulls out a fraction and pushes back gently. My inner muscles clench in an effort to expel the cause of my pain. He curses under his breath, sweat beading on his forehead.

"You're going to make me come before I'm fully inside you," he says with a tight jaw.

It sounds like a reprimand, but I don't know what he wants from me. I moan when he moves again, and it's not a sound of pleasure.

"Relax, *ma cherie*," he says. "Take a deep breath for me."

I do, and it helps a little.

"That's good." He kisses my cheek. "Like that."

Just as the tension in my muscles ease marginally, he surges forward, driving past the barrier that prevents his entry. My inner muscles protest. It feels as if he's tearing me apart. The stretch is unbearable, the pain white-hot. I forget to breathe. My lips part on a soundless gasp.

Maxime stills. His entire body tenses on top of mine. His gaze goes wide. Shock settles in the winter-gray pools and bleeds into male pride.

"Ah, Zoe." He clicks his tongue and shakes his head, but possessive satisfaction burns in his eyes. "You should've told me."

Unbidden tears gather in my eyes. I try to blink them away, but they spill over when I lower my lashes.

He kisses the corner of my eye, his lips tracing the path of my tears. "I would've prepared you better."

Him having this knowledge only makes it worse.

"Don't cry." His big hands cup my jaw, holding my head carefully. "I'll take care of you."

He moved as he spoke, his shallow thrusts making the burn flare. I dig my nails into the fabric of his shirt, clutching his arms as he punishes me with every roll of his hips, but then his lips are on mine. The kiss is sweet and tender. It somehow settles me as his hands find their way to my breasts, his fingers brushing softly over my nipples. They harden, and the pleasure his touch elicits echoes in my clit.

The burn doesn't abate, but I turn slicker. He presses deeper, his entry slightly easier. The more he kisses me, the more my body softens around him until he's fully sheathed and our groins press together.

"Zoe," he says into my mouth, his voice drenched in arousal.

I can only cling to him as he lets me get used to the feeling for a moment before increasing his pace. He releases my mouth and pulls away to look at my face. Pushing up on one arm, he slips a hand between our bodies. When his fingers find my clit, the pleasure of earlier returns, the need I'm now familiar with rising above the hurt and somehow diminishing the pain.

"That's my girl," he says.

I don't want to touch him, but as the pleasure climbs, and I'm spiraling out of control I need to hold onto something. My arms go around him of their own accord, finding an anchor in his strong body.

He starts moving faster, and my body follows instinctively. He groans when I wrap my legs around him in an automatic move to hold on. The pain is still there, but I don't register it any longer. I only feel the tension of the building release I need like food or water. I'm almost at the crescendo when he pulls out of me violently. I cry out in discomfort.

Reaching over me for the nightstand drawer, he takes out a condom, and tears the packet open with his teeth. I can't believe I didn't think about protection in my haze of lust. When he sits back on his heels to fit the condom, I look at his cock. He's covered in my blood and arousal. The sheets are a mess. My cheeks heat in shame of how badly I want him to finish this, how badly I need this from a man I hate.

After rolling on the condom, he pushes back inside me. A perverse part of me mourns the loss of his naked skin and resents the new barrier. Then all thoughts fly from my head as he pushes deep and slides almost all the way out before burying deep again. The movement strokes over nerve endings, adding new pleasure to the familiar. He massages my clit in slow circles as he takes me with an increasingly demanding pace. Only when my body starts to tighten and the pleasure reaches a new height does he lose his control.

He moves harder, chasing his own release faster. I moan, the sounds coming from my mouth belonging to a wanton woman. When my orgasm explodes, he throws back his head on a low groan, driving himself as deep into me as he can. His body hardens, his muscles growing taught under my palms. I can feel the knots and grooves of the maleness that defines his back under his shirt. He drops his head next to mine, breathing hard.

Turning his face a fraction, he plants a soft kiss on my temple. "You'll be my destruction."

I sag back, letting the mattress absorb my weight.

He's already my destruction.

I'm no longer the woman I used to be.

I can never go back to how things were.

CHAPTER 11

Zoe

When Maxime rolls off me, I push up onto my arms. My thighs are covered in blood, much more than I expected there'd be. The sheets are soiled. Traces of my lost virginity mark the white fabric of Maxime's shirt. He scans my face as he removes the condom. I need to escape that piercing stare. The invasion of my body was enough. I don't want him digging through my feelings.

He gets up and walks to the bathroom. The moment the door closes, I'm on my feet. I have to escape this bed. I want to run, but the lounge is as far as I can go. The ache between my legs is persistent, an unpleasant reminder of my new reality.

I go straight to the wet bar and pour myself a whiskey. I'm not a big drinker, and I've never had whiskey, but I down the shot in one go. It steals my breath, burning all the way to my stomach. Spotting the packet of cigarettes next to the decanter, I snatch it up with the lighter and look around the room for something to wear. I'm not going back to the bedroom. Not yet. My gaze falls on the clotheshorse with Maxime's tux jacket. I don't give it a second thought. I pull the jacket on and push the sliding door wide open, not caring that the cold blasts inside or that my body feels frozen the minute I step barefoot onto the terrace.

I light a cigarette and inhale deeply. My gaze is trained on the beautiful view, the reflection of the streetlights in the water, but I don't really see it. My thoughts are trained inward. They're turbulent. How do I reconcile the woman I became in that bed with the one I used to be? How could I find pleasure at the hands of a man I loathe? Because he was gentle? A good lover? Considerate? Because he did everything right?

My fingers curl into a ball at that admission. It would've been easier and less confusing if he was cruel. I don't know how to place the man, and I need to know. He's my enemy. An unpredictable enemy is the most dangerous kind. I don't understand him, and that scares me. I don't understand his actions or motivations.

A shadow stretches over the floor. Maxime steps up next to me, dressed in tracksuit pants and a T-shirt. I don't turn my head to acknowledge him. I keep my gaze trained on the water and the lights, an image as pretty as it is traitorous, because I know what ugliness lies underneath the foundations of this city.

He takes the cigarette from my fingers. I only notice now how much I'm shaking and how my teeth are chattering from the cold. I sense him looking at me. I'm aware of him, no longer lost in my head, but I don't look at him or acknowledge his existence.

He takes a drag before putting the cigarette out in the ashtray. "Do you smoke?"

"No." I experimented a little after school but decided I didn't like it. "Do you?"

"No."

My question was meant to be sarcastic, but his answer surprises me, and even more so his placating tone. Leaning my elbows on the rail, I finally turn to face him. The jacket falls open, but I don't care. I don't care that I'm cold. I welcome the frozen numbness of my body. I don't care that he sees. He's seen it all. There's nothing left to give.

The wind blows his fringe over his forehead. He must be cold, but he just stands there quietly, watching me. It infuriates me. I want him to talk, to tell me why I'm here, to explain this twisted game he's playing.

"Why did you do it?" I ask.

He dips his head, his stance casual but his eyes sharp and aware. "Do what?"

"The dress, the flowers, the opera…the extravagant dinner. Why?"

His gaze is level. "For the same reason I brought you here."

"You've already done the convincing role-play for Damian's sake yesterday. You didn't have to repeat it today."

"I could've done that anywhere."

I still. I've had it figured out. Didn't I? If not to convince my brother I was here out of my own free will, a loved and pampered woman, then why? I will him to speak, to say it, but he's keeping that little distance between us, waiting patiently for me to connect the dots.

"I don't get it," I finally say.

His monotone voice is flat, a robot conveying facts. Or maybe reserved, as if he's not sure how I'm going to take this. "To give you your fantasy."

The words bowl me over. For a moment, I still don't understand, but then, slowly, the meaning sinks in. Oh, my God. My chest constricts. It hurts to breathe. He didn't bring me here to show my friends and Damian how lucky and happy I am. Maybe that too, but that was just a convenient bonus.

My lips part in shock. "You brought me here to fuck me." Because he knows my most intimate ideals. He knows about Venice, my fixation with this particular opera house, and my version of the perfect dress. He stole my life and my dream, mixed them together in some fucked-up fantasy, and served them to me in a twisted version of reality. He knows my desires and used them against me. "You son of a bitch. You used my dream to create this whole romantic little scenario."

His regard remains cautious. "Would you have preferred the crueler version?"

"I prefer the truth."

He closes the two steps between us. Grabbing the lapels of the jacket, he brings the edges together to cover my body. "Is that why you didn't tell me, Zoe? Because you prefer the truth?"

I look away.

His tone is gentle, one you'd use trying to coax the truth out of someone. "Why were you still a virgin?"

"I was waiting for the right man," I say like it doesn't matter.

He nods, a silent acknowledgment of understanding. There's no remorse in his voice when he says, "No man can be more wrong than me."

I'm shaking violently when he picks me up, sheltering me against his chest. He carries me inside and easily closes the door balancing me in one arm. He goes to the bathroom and lowers me onto the rug next to the bath. I wrap my arms around myself, shivering as I watch him open the tap to let the water run warm. The petals and candles are gone. The bath has been cleaned. Housekeeping came in while we were having dinner.

The bath is only a quarter full when he slips his palms under the jacket and brushes it off my shoulders, carelessly disregarding the expensive garment crumpled on the floor. He picks me up and puts me on my feet in the bath. Taking a jar of bath salts from the edge, he empties the whole jar in the bath and scoops water into the jar that he empties over my shoulder.

The warmth dispels the cold. My skin contracts with goosebumps. He refills the jar and drains it over my other shoulder. He does the same with my front and back, and then he crouches down to soap a sponge. He starts at my waist, dragging the sponge from my hip to my thigh before squeezing out the sponge and letting the soapy water run down my calf. Meticulously, he washes me, stroke by gentle stroke removing the blood and the cold.

The bathroom is warm, but I'm still shivering. When the bath is half-full, he turns off the water and guides me to lie down. Twisting my hair in a knot, he trails it over the edge of the bath. The water stings between my legs, but heat envelopes me, melting the last of the bitter frost under my skin and calming my shivers. All the while, he continues to bathe me, washing away the remnants of our coupling in a strangely humble way as if I'm the princess and he the servant.

When my skin starts to wrinkle, he pulls the plug and takes my hand to help me out of the bath. Draping a fluffy towel around me, he dries my body. When not a patch of wetness is left on my skin, he leads me back to the room and makes me sit on the loveseat while he strips the sheets off the bed, leaving the duvet. Folding it back, he looks at me in silent command.

I'm spent. My fight is cold. I get up without arguing, dropping the towel at the side of the bed before getting in. Turning on my side, I face the wall. He gets in beside me, flicks off the lamp, and spoons me from behind with an arm he throws over my stomach to anchor me to him.

Our breathing is quiet. We're both awake, but neither of us speaks. Light from the streetlamps falls through the window into the room. It plays over the walls, creating a shadowed reflection of the free world outside.

After a long while, he says into the darkness, "If I had the time, I would've made you fall in love with me first."

At the words, I stop breathing.

They're meant to be a consolation, but they're stunningly cruel.

CHAPTER 12

Maxime

The day is gray, the Mistral blowing at full force when we land in Marseille. It was a bumpy flight and a rough landing, but my pilot is skilled. A car is waiting when we exit the plane, Alexis leaning against it. I'm not fooled into seeing it as a one-man welcoming committee. My brother isn't here for me. He looks beyond me at the woman who stiffly descends the steps. His curiosity is palpable and his excitement sickening.

In an impulsive, possessive act, I find Zoe's hand and close my fingers around hers. Alexis's gaze homes in on the gesture. His face folds into a frown as he takes in her fashionable wool coat and patent leather boots.

He straightens as we approach. Not sparing Zoe another glance, he addresses me in French. "What's going on, Max?"

My smile is fake. "You tell me." My cousin, Jerome, informed me that Alexis negotiated a deal with the Italians.

He watches me with the attention of a hawk. "Why is our hostage wearing Gucci?"

My voice betrays my tension. "She's no longer our hostage."

He lifts a brow. "You were supposed to hand her over to me."

"The plan has changed."

"To what? The whore is now our guest?"

I narrow my eyes. My tone is quiet but the violence underneath anything but. "Mind your mouth. She's my mistress."

He laughs softly, shaking his head. "You're something else, Max. Father won't be pleased."

I open the car door for Zoe. "Does it look like I give a damn?"

"No, you don't. That's part of the problem, isn't it?"

It's not the first time he accuses me of putting my selfish needs before the business. He's a hypocrite. Alexis has never done anything unless it benefits him.

"Why?" he asks. "Does she have a golden cunt?"

I'm not going to let that remark slide, but I'm not taking him on in front of Benoit and Gautier who are following with our luggage. Alexis will own up to his filthy tongue later.

I keep my smile intact. "Jealous?"

He turns his attention back to Zoe, looking her over as if she's livestock. "Nah. She's not much for the eye. Too thick around the hips for my liking."

That's because he hasn't been in her space, hasn't seen her hopeless faith and quiet resilience. He'd crush a pretty little flower under his two-thousand-dollar moccasins and never even notice it.

"Shut up and drive." I add mockingly, "Isn't that why you're here?"

He grins, not taking the bait, and shifts to behind the wheel.

Benoit and Gautier load our suitcases into the trunk before making their way to the hangar where we keep a couple of cars. They'll follow.

We don't talk on the way home. I keep holding onto Zoe's hand, feeling her tense as we turn through the gates of my property forty-five minutes later. The house stands on an acre of land on the outskirts of Cassis. It's built on the edge of the cliff, overlooking the sea.

Alexis parks in the front but doesn't get out. "Welcome home, brother. I'm not going to hang around for the victory drinks."

Ignoring his mocking tone, I get out and open Zoe's door. A guard rushes over from his post by the entrance to take our bags from the trunk. Zoe looks up at the two-story mansion with its double chimneys, shutters, and ivy-covered walls. I try to look at it through her eyes, try to see what she sees. It's a typical southern French design, the house dating from four centuries back. I went to great pains to restore it, as well as with the design of the formal garden and its maze. It must be unfamiliar and strange, not what she's used to.

The front door opens just as Alexis pulls off. My mother exits, wearing her cooking apron over a Chanel dress. As always, she's impeccably groomed, her white-gray hair styled into a bob and her makeup cleverly invisible. Despite her age, her face is youthful, a lucky trait she's inherited from her long line of purebred aristocracy.

"Max." Her features light up with a smile that freezes when she notices the woman at my side. Her mouth draws down. It's minute, quickly replaced with a friendly expression, but I noticed. I know her too well.

She pulls herself to her full petite height, her spine going stiff. "I cooked. I reckoned you'd be hungry. God only knows what you had to eat in that godforsaken country. I didn't expect you to come home with a guest." She looks at Zoe. "There won't be enough food."

"Never mind, Maman." I kiss her cheeks. "We'll make do." I switch over to English. "This is Zoe. Zoe, this is my mother, Cecile."

My mother doesn't kiss Zoe's cheeks, but offers her hand, a gesture that demeans Zoe for a lower class but that someone not familiar with our culture won't grasp.

Zoe glances at me. I give a small nod, a warning, at which she shakes my mother's hand. My mother isn't up to speed with the grittier details of our business, even if she knows how we conduct it is shady. My father prefers to keep her in the dark, to protect her as he claims, not only from the blood on our hands, but also from his mistresses. If my mother knows, she's never given on, but her reaction to Zoe tells me she may be less ignorant about my father's infidelity than what I've thought, or, for her sake, hoped.

"Well," my mother says in English, her accent worse than mine, "you better come in."

She steps aside for us to enter. The guard follows with the suitcases.

"Where must I put this, sir?" he asks in French.

"In my bedroom."

My mother purses her lips. Her gaze flicks over Zoe's pleated coat and killer heel boots with distaste.

As I help Zoe from her coat, my mother, reverting back to French, asks, "How long is she staying?"

I put the coat on the stand by the door before removing my own. "A while."

Her silence communicates her displeasure.

"You didn't have to come out all the way here to cook for me," I say.

She pinches my cheek. "I'm your mother. That's my job."

"In English, please."

She irons out her apron and switches back to English. "Go freshen up. Lunch will be ready when you're done."

I show Zoe to the guest bathroom downstairs and wait outside.

When she exits, I take her arm, squeezing harder than necessary. "Not a word to my mother or anyone for that matter. Say anything out of line, and Damian pays the price. Understand?"

She stares at up me, her big, blue eyes shimmering with apprehension and a twist of hostility. "Yes."

"Good." I kiss the top of her head just because I can and lead her to the dining room.

Her arm brushes against mine as we walk. I'm overly aware of her, my usual business-focused mind distracted. I don't know many twenty-one-year-old virgins. I never could've guessed. The knowledge surges in me with heated satisfaction. Her innocence suits me even better. I've never liked to share my toys as a child. That hasn't changed once I turned into an adult. If anything, the trait became more imbedded in my making. I guess Alexis is right. I am a selfish bastard.

My mother waits at the table, her apron removed and the rings she takes off for cooking back on her fingers. The five-carat emerald surrounded by diamonds is a family ring, passed on for generations from mother to daughter. We don't have a sister. Alexis and I are the only children. As the first-born, the ring will be passed on to my wife, and I know exactly what my mother is thinking as she twists the ring on her finger while studying Zoe with a tight expression.

I seat Zoe on my right and take the head of the table. My mother already sits on the left, a place normally reserved for the lady of the house. A veal roast with Parisian potatoes and green beans are set out. There's enough to feed ten people.

"It smells delicious," I say, taking the carving knife.

"Your favorite." My mother gives me a tender look, a look that speaks of family intimacy and customs, one that excludes outsiders such as Zoe. Our clan has always been a clique.

After I've carved the meat, my mother serves while I pour the wine. She fills me in on the watering of the plants she's managed in my absence, which ones have flowered, and the groceries she's ordered to be delivered. We talk about my cousins, Sylvie and Noelle, who will be home soon from the university they attend in Paris.

"I got you some tangerines," my mother says after we've finished the main course, pushing the bowl toward me. "They're the ones from Corsica you like so much."

"You shouldn't have gone to so much trouble." I take one, peel it, and place it on Zoe's plate. "I have a cook, you know."

My mother sniffs. "She doesn't know you like I do. Neither does she cook like me." She pushes to her feet. "I've been in the kitchen on my feet all morning. I need a break."

I stand. "Who's driving you?"

"One of your father's men."

I kiss her cheeks. "Thank you for lunch."

She pats my arm. "Take care of yourself." To Zoe, she says, "Goodbye, then."

Zoe mumbles a barely audible greeting.

"Have some tea," I say to Zoe. In other words, stay.

I see my mother out.

While pulling her coat and scarf on at the entrance, she asks, "How did you meet this…" she waves a hand, "…whatever her name is?"

"Zoe. By chance."

My mother fits her gloves. "She's a foreigner, Max."

"I'm well aware, Maman."

"Is she Catholic?"

"You know I'm not religious."

She sighs and pats my cheek. "I have to be home before the charity meeting this afternoon. Do think about making a donation. Those poor kids can do with the aid."

"I'll write a check."

"Good."

I signal the guard waiting on a bench next to my father's Mercedes and walk my mother to the car.

My mother hesitates when I open the door. "Max, you know how this is going to look."

I feel one of those long talks coming. "I'm thirty, not ten."

Sighing again, she gets inside and waves as the driver pulls off. I lift a hand in greeting, waiting until they clear the gates before going back inside.

I find Zoe in the dining room where I left her, a teacup in her hand. She looks up when I enter, her expression uncertain.

"Come," I say. "I'll show you the bedroom."

The way she tenses gives me the same jabbing sensation in my chest as when she showed me so openly how repulsive the idea of me fucking her is. My face may put her off, but she had pleasure last night. She may hate the idea, but she liked what I did to her. In time, she'll get used to looking at me.

We go upstairs to the master suite. I open the door and usher her inside. The room is spacious with a sitting area and dressing room that connects to the bathroom. The French doors open onto a balcony. The view is magnificent. She goes to the window to look out at the sea. I'm proud. My home is more than an investment. It's the only place I can let my guard down and relax.

"What do you think?" I really want to know. Why it's important to me that she likes my home I don't know.

She turns on me, ire shining in her pretty, blue eyes. "What do you want me to say? That it's lovely? That my prison is beautiful? Shall I swoon over how big and fancy your property is, over how much it's worth?"

I give her a warning look. "A simple thank you will do."

"Oh, my mistake. I guess this is the part where I thank you for saving me from being locked up and raped."

I let it go. She's tired. She's been through a lot in the last three days, especially last night. "If you need anything, my housekeeper, Francine, will see to your needs. My home is yours, and I won't go out of my way to make you miserable."

I step closer. "However, don't make the mistake of thinking I'm a forgiving man. You will act your part, or Damian pays. If you run, your brother is dead. Live by my rules, and we'll get on fine. It doesn't have to be unpleasant for you. If you try, I'm sure you'll like living here."

Her look is cutting. What the hell am I doing? I took on a mountain of problems for myself by claiming Zoe. I could've just handed a faceless, nameless, meaningless woman over to my brother, just another pawn in a strategy to protect our business. No, I had to make it personal. I had to see her for who she is. I allowed her to fascinate me. I allowed her secrets to tempt me. Whatever the case, no matter how ungrateful she is or how much she hates me, I can't go back on my decision. After last night, it's much too late for that now.

I cup her cheek, giving her affection, because that's what she needs. "I'll be back tonight. Feel free to look around the house, but don't go outside. In case you're tempted, I have guards stationed on the grounds and at the gate. If you get hungry, Francine will fix you a snack."

I kiss the top of her head and walk away before I'm tempted to strip her naked and do more. Leaving her alone so soon isn't ideal, but facing my father is a bigger priority.

After giving my guards instructions not to let her off the property, I leave a note for Francine, who is out on her lunch break. My guest isn't allowed to use the telephones. I unplug all the landlines and lock them in my study. Then I take one of the cars in the garage, preferring to drive. I need to think, and I'd rather be alone.

On the way to Marseille, I consider how to present the decision to my father. He won't be happy, especially not now that our negotiations with the Italians have started. He'd want no complications, nothing to interfere with the fragile business development.

My father's office is near the harbor. I pull up front and throw the keys to the valet to park the car. Raphael Belshaw sits on his throne behind his desk when I enter. His thick, gray hair is brushed back, the waves neatly tamed. As always, he's dressed in a black suit and white shirt. My uncle, Emile, my father's younger brother, sits in the visitor's chair.

My father looks at me through narrowed eyes, the left one drooping. "You're late."

His displeasure isn't about the hour. I bet Alexis wasted no time in sharing the news.

"Bad weather. We had to circle for a while before we could land." I bend down to hug my uncle and slap his back in the habitual way of greeting. "How are Sylvie and Noelle?"

He scoffs. "Spending too much money in Paris."

"At least they're getting a good education."

My uncle raps his fingers on the desktop, the gold ring with our family crest knocking against the wood. "I don't know why they bother. They'll marry and have babies. What good is a career going to do them, then? If you ask me, they're only throwing money into the water."

I take the seat next to him. "Some women like to work, just like men."

He stands. "Times have changed, and I'm not sure it's for the better." He nods at my father. "I'll leave you to catch up with Max. Don't forget Hadrienne is organizing a lunch on Sunday to welcome the girls home from Paris. We expect you all to be there." He takes his hat from the coat stand. "You included, Max."

The minute the door closes behind him, my father says, "You have some fucking explaining to do."

I give a wry smile. "Ah, Alexis stopped by."

"Alexis said you took Damian's sister as a mistress. Tell me it's a joke."

"I'd never play a joke like that."

My father leans forward, his gaze harsh. "Then what are you playing at, son?"

"Damian Hart may be behind bars, but he's powerful and becoming more so by the day. He's snide, clever, merciless, and resourceful. He's wasted no time in making the right kind of connections on the inside. He's got people looking out for him on the outside, managing the money he earns by getting information and doing dirty jobs. He can't put his hands on that money now, but he will be able to when they let him out in two years." My father knows money and connections mean power, enough to start a war. "We don't want him for an enemy."

"Wasn't that the point of taking his sister? Tell me how that doesn't make him our enemy."

"The point was having something to hold over his head." To blackmail him into honoring our deal with Dalton when the ownership of the mine transfers to Hart. "This way will be even better."

My father grumbles. "Better how?"

"He'll honor the deal if his sister is happy. If he thinks she's here because she wants to be, he'll want to make sure she continues to be happy, and we won't have to fight a war." One we may very well lose.

He gives me a skeptical look. "How do you expect to pull that one off?"

It's simple, really. "By making her happy."

His belly shakes with a laugh. "We kidnapped her. How is that going to make her happy?"

"I have my ways. The idea will grow on her."

"The chances of you two meeting accidentally are too big a coincidence." My father interlaces his fingers on the tabletop. "Hart won't fall for it."

"I already thought about it." On the drive over, in fact. "I went to South Africa to meet Dalton about business. We talked about the mine, and I asked how the diamond deposit was discovered. We've had a couple of bottles of wine, so he told me about Damian Hart, the discoverer, who ended up in jail for stealing a diamond from Dalton's house during a dinner party. I was curious. Something about the story didn't add up. Why would Hart steal a diamond if he's discovered a whole riverbed full of them? So, I visited Hart's only remaining family, Zoe Hart, to hear her opinion of the story. We went out for dinner. There was an instant attraction, and I decided to save her from her miserable life and give her a better one."

He sneers. "You're a fucking Hallmark movie director now? You think you've got it all figured out, don't you?"

I cross my legs. "I do."

His nostrils flare. His fingers curl around the Montblanc pen on his desk, squeezing so hard that thick, blue veins pop out on his hand. I bet he'd love to stab me with that pen. I've often wondered if there'd come a day I'd shove him over that edge. I've always pushed his buttons by being the defiant son, the one who doesn't follow orders. I guess that's why he prefers Alexis. Alexis doesn't pose questions. As long as it's for the business, and therefore for himself, Alexis does what he's told. He's easier to handle, not unimpressionable like me, and a lot more like my father. Which makes me my mother's favorite. She doesn't hate my father, but she doesn't exactly love him, either. Alexis reminds her too much of Raphael Belshaw, the man she wedded as a business arrangement. I wouldn't say Maman loves Alexis less, but she's always treated me differently, favoring me.

The skin on my father's brow plows into grooves as his mind

works at full speed, but there's no way out of this. A lover is a lover, entitled to protection and a certain amount of respect. You can't mess with the unspoken rules of *les beaux voyous* without upturning the apple cart.

He slams a fist on the desk. "Why couldn't Alexis make her *happy*?"

He says *happy* like it's a curse, and my whole body snaps tight at the mere thought of that. I'm unable to filter all the anger from my voice. "We both know Alexis isn't capable of making anyone happy, let alone an unwilling woman. We both know, too, how it would've turned out for Zoe if Alexis took her. That would've definitely made Hart our enemy. He would've sent an army to save her. He wouldn't have stopped until he destroyed us."

"What about the Italians? We can't afford any complications now."

"We'll be discreet." I add a jibe. "Just like you are."

His droopy eye twitches. "What prevents her from running or telling her brother?"

"She doesn't know why we took her. I told her if she runs or tries anything Hart will pay." Of course, we have no intention of harming Hart. We need him to revive the mine or our business will sink, anyway.

"In other words, you're blackmailing *her* instead of us blackmailing Hart."

"Genius, no?"

He leans back, his words sounding bitter with unwilling acceptance. "I suppose it's easier to manipulate the girl."

"She's young. Hart is worldly and hardy."

He drums his fingers on the desk, considering my words. He's unwilling to admit it, but he doesn't have a choice. If we take a family vote on the decision, he'll lose. Half of the power of running the business has already transferred to me at my thirtieth birthday, like it had to my father, and his father, and every other Belshaw before him. The other half I'll get when I marry. My father is a loose cannon. He's made too many bad decisions. His love for overindulgence and unnecessary violence has stained our reputation and name. The family likes the stability I bring to the business. They'll vote for me.

After a while, he says, "Fine. You have two years to tame her before Hart gets out."

I stand. "That's doable."

"You better hope so. If this backfires—"

"It won't backfire."

He grimaces. "We'll see. Now get out of here. I have work to do."

"Where's Alexis?"

"Overseeing the docks."

I straighten my tie. "I'll see you on Sunday."

I GET my car and drive to the end of the docking area where the debt collectors hang around, playing cards. Alexis is having a conversation with one of the men.

Walking up to my brother with brisk strides, I say, "A word with you."

He saunters around the corner, his hands in his pockets. The minute he turns back to me, I slam my fist into his face. His head bounces back, hitting the wall. Blood pours from his nose.

Grabbing his nose between his hands, he gives me an incredulous look. "What the fuck, Max?"

"That," I point a finger at him, "is for mentioning Zoe's cunt."

"Are you fucking crazy?" He fumbles for the decorative handkerchief in his top jacket pocket and presses it against his nose. "You just said it yourself."

"Only me." I stab his chest with the finger I was waving in his face. "I'm the only one who mentions, breathes, fucks, and eats out Zoe's cunt. I'm the only one who thinks about her cunt. Get it?"

He raises his palms. "Calm the fuck down, man."

Now that I've put him back in his place, I am calm. The problem with being part of the family is that if you don't enforce the rules, every dick like my brother will try to break them. If I can't stand up for what's mine, no one will respect my property. It's an important lesson. No one will fuck with Zoe after this.

I turn and walk back down the road that stinks of diesel and fish.

"You're fucking nuts," Alexis calls after me.

I don't look back. Doing so would mean I care about the insult. Alexis's laughter follows me into the car. I start the engine and clench the wheel. I should be going to the office in the city. I should catch up with the Italian deal. Instead, I turn the car in the opposite direction.

I need a vent for my anger, and my vent is at home.

CHAPTER 13

Zoe

The moment I hear the front door shut, I go to the writing desk standing in the far corner of Maxime's room and go through it. I find what I'm looking for in the second drawer. Pulling out the writing pad and pen, I sit down in the chair and write a letter to Damian.

I tell him I've arrived safely in France after a short holiday in Italy. I tell him Venice was magical. I tell him I'm settling in nicely in my new home, baking apple pie. I tell him I can't wait for the day he gets out, that I'll bake apple pie to welcome him, and I hope he'll bring his cell mate for me to meet. I'm sure his friend will love apple pie. I make sure to mention the address and give a detailed description of the property. I paid attention to the road signs on the way and the address on the letterbox by the gate. I mention how wealthy and important my white knight is, so much so that his property is guarded. Then I sign off as always, my name with two x's and o's.

To anyone reading it, it's just a letter from a happy girl who got lucky by landing a rich guy, but Damian will understand the code. He'll get the message. He'll know Zane and Maxime are his enemies, and that I'm being held against my will.

Folding the letter neatly, I seal it in an envelope I find in the same drawer and write the address on it. Then I go through the room, looking for a phone. I doubt Maxime would've left one, which is why my priority was writing the letter, but I still try.

There are no landline plugs in the room, so I take the letter and exit onto the landing. The house is quiet. No sounds come from the kitchen. The hallway is dark and spooky. Faded tapestries and portraits of men and women dressed in clothes from centuries ago hang on the walls. The space smells of wood polish and cedar. I shudder but force myself to walk out onto the creaking wooden floor, opening doors as far as I go.

The one next to Max's room gives access to a bedroom the same size as his but decorated with feminine pinks and lilacs. The two rooms share the same bathroom and balcony. The other rooms on the floor are all bedrooms with en-suite bathrooms. A heavy wooden door at the end of the hallway gives access to a spiral staircase. Unable to squash my curiosity, I climb the stone steps to the top. The staircase exits into a circular tower room. A narrow bay window with a built-in bench overlooks the sea. I can't make out much of the view through the stained-glass window. The only furniture is a small desk. Other than that, the floor and walls are bare. It's cold and noisy with the wind cutting around the tower.

Shivering, I go back to the first-floor landing and descend the steps to the foyer. I pass the guest bathroom and dining room, a big and smaller lounge, and am about to reach for the door at the end when it opens in my face.

Gasping, I clutch the letter to my chest. A woman dressed in dark slacks and a button-down blouse stops dead when she sees me. Her green eyes widen. She sweeps her gaze over me, taking in my face, clothes, and boots. Slender and willowy, she's a head taller than me. Her blond hair is twisted into a bun, and her smooth skin is pale like porcelain, but unlike mine, hers is blemish free. She's wearing mascara and a glossy pink lipstick. Her perfume is faint but smells expensive.

"Oh," she says, "you must be Zoe." Her accent is less pronounced than Maxime's.

"You must be Francine."

"I just got back from my lunch break and found Max's note." She gives me another quick once-over. "Is there something you wanted?"

I hand her the letter. "I was hoping someone could mail this for me. I don't have a stamp."

She reaches for it hesitantly. "I'll leave it with Max's mail. He usually drops it in the mailbox on his way to work."

My spirits sink. He'll read it, no doubt. He won't understand the hidden messages, but he may not like the details I conveyed about his house, such as how well protected it is and where it's situated. I can only hope he won't burn it.

For a moment, I hold onto the envelope, reluctant to hand it over, but when Francine pulls a little, I have no choice. I have to let go if I don't want to give her a reason to be suspicious.

"If there's nothing else?" She folds her arms, the envelope clutched in one hand. She's posed like a ballerina, one knee bent with her foot turned out and her long fingers resting elegantly on the sleeve on her blouse. Her nails are painted with a French manicure.

"No, thanks."

"If you'll excuse me, I have to start dinner."

"Of course."

Going back inside the kitchen, she closes the door. She might've well put a sign on it that reads *stay out*.

Not knowing what else to do with myself, I go through the rest of the house. Every room is decorated with antique furniture. There's even a knight's armor and medieval weapons. The place is like a museum. I don't find a phone anywhere, and the empty wall plug in the entrance indicates the phone has been unplugged. I would've given anything to call Damian now, to tell him what my letter may not convey if Maxime decides not to send it.

One of the doors is locked, presumably a room Maxime doesn't want me to have access to, and next to it I find a library with a fireplace. The house is cold. My wool dress barely keeps me warm. I use the chopped wood stacked in the basket to build a fire and stoke it until the flames leap high. To my dismay, all the books are in French. I settle on one about the region with photographs and drag the armchair closer to the fire.

In no time, my cold muscles thaw. My face warms, and my fingers prick with pins and needles as the frozen stiffness melts away. A gust of wind enters as the front door opens across the foyer. Maxime stands on the step, looking windblown and angry.

The physical heat remains, but a blast of coldness settles over me when he closes the door. My stomach tightens with apprehension as he removes his coat, scarf, and gloves, and hangs everything neatly on the coat stand before making his way to the library. I'm in full sight of the open door, and he watches me darkly as he advances.

I shut the book when he enters. My mouth goes dry when he closes the door and turns the key. I'm uncertain of him. I can't place him. I don't know who he is right now, the man of the cold cell or the man of the luxurious hotel suite.

CHAPTER 14

Maxime

Working my tie loose, I walk to the chair where Zoe is draped so prettily and stop in front of her. I'm hard. I want her. I've never wanted with such abandon. Certainly not a woman. My dirty pleasures are money and power. Sex is a recreational activity, a form of release. I enjoy it, but I enjoy work more. Not today, it seems. Today I chose her over the office, and I do need release.

As I take the book from her hand and leave it on the coffee table, I blame Alexis. I blame my anger as I pull her to her feet and take her place on the chair. It's warm, her body heat lingering in the flowery upholstery.

I unbutton my jacket and cross my legs. I rest my hands on the armrests, a casual pose that belies how badly I want to lay them on her. I trail my gaze over her, taking in her luscious curves before pausing on the pussy at my eye level, the cunt I've assaulted my brother over.

"Sore?" I ask, lifting my eyes back to hers.

She stares down at me with her beautiful face, the pink flush on her cheeks from the fire deepening to a red. "Yes."

I can't take her again so soon, but there are other ways. "Undress."

Her blue eyes go wide. "What?"

"Take off your clothes."

She inhales audibly. "Why?"

I raise a brow.

Her curls tumble over her shoulders as she shakes her head. "I don't want to have sex."

"I won't fuck you with my cock, but I did say often and convincingly."

Her hands fist into the skirt of her dress. "It hurts."

"I'm not going to hurt you."

"I didn't enjoy it."

My little liar. "You came, didn't you?"

"That doesn't mean I liked it."

I cock a shoulder. "You don't have to come if you don't want."

"Then why do it?"

"That's what lovers do."

"Get naked in the study?"

My lips twitch. "Anywhere I want. You better get used to it, Zoe. These are the games grownups play."

Her dainty nostrils flare. "Fuck you. I'm inexperienced. That doesn't make me a child."

"We're going to punish that mouth of yours, but first things first. Are you going to undress, or do you find it more romantic if I undress you?"

She glares at me with her dress bunched in her tiny fists.

"It's my job to teach you how to please me, and apparently also yourself, but I'm not going to force you."

"But we are going to sleep together," she says, a glint of rebellion in her eyes.

"Naturally. Unless you've changed your mind?"

"No," she says, unclenching her fingers. "I haven't changed my mind."

"Then trust me."

"Trust you?" She laughs.

"Trust me with your body. I know what I'm doing."

"You certainly have the experience," she throws back at me. "Don't you?"

Bringing up my experience isn't going to help win her over. "You're the most important person in this room. Only your needs matter."

"I don't have needs."

Such a wordy little girl. "Are you going to trust me? You're only wasting your own time. Whether today, tomorrow, or next week, you will take off your clothes for me and ask me to make you come."

She narrows her eyes. "I won't ask to come."

My smile holds a challenge. "Prove it."

She glares at me some more but does reach for the zipper of her dress at her back. I don't offer to help. I sit and watch. That's my job. It's showing her how lovely she is.

She pulls the zipper down and pushes the dress from her shoulders and over her hips. Her underwear is chocolate-brown, the same color as the dress. It's lacy and pretty, but I prefer her naked. She removes the boots and stockings, and then the underwear.

Standing naked in front of me, she asks bitingly, "I'm supposed to need this?"

I take in her firm breasts and pink nipples, her narrow waist, and curved hips. The dark, unshaven triangle between her legs. She's voluptuous, small but rounded where it matters. "You're very beautiful, Zoe."

The pink of her cheeks flares again. "What now, Maxime?"

"Come sit on my lap and tell my what you did while I was away."

Her lips part. "What?"

"You heard me."

She pads over uncertainly. When she stops in front of me, I

uncross my legs and spread them. Turning sideways, she steps between them. I hook my hands under her arms to lift her onto my thigh, arranging her with her legs draped over the armrest and her back in the crook of my arm.

I brush her curls over her shoulder before trailing my fingers down her arm, keeping the touch light. "Did you explore the house?"

Goosebumps break out over her skin. "Yes."

I drag my fingers up to her shoulder and back down to her wrist. "Do you like it?" Up, down, and up again. "And no more sass like earlier."

She shivers a little. "What do you want me to say? You have a nice house. A little spooky, but impressive."

I smile at the spooky bit, tracing the arch of her neck. "It has a great view. Have you looked outside?"

She turns her face to me. "You told me I wasn't allowed to go outside."

I explore the elegant curve of her collarbone with my fingertips. "On the balcony."

"No, but I went up in the tower."

"Mm." I brush the back of my knuckles over a pink nipple. The tip hardens. The darker skin around contracts. "I don't go there much, but women seem drawn to it. It must be the princess in the tower thing."

She stiffens. "I was just curious. I didn't go up there with some repressed fantasy."

I place my palm on her waist, the touch meant to be calming. "That's not what I said."

"No, what you said is that you bring many women here."

"You're the only one here now, aren't you?"

She doesn't answer.

I bring my hand back to her breast, stroking the underside with a thumb. "Did you meet Fran?"

"Yes." She leans her full weight against me, settling in deeper. "She speaks English very well. She almost doesn't have an accent."

I move to the other breast, tracing the areola with a finger. The tip buds beautifully, growing hard even before I flick a finger over it. "She studied at a culinary school in London. Her food is very good. I'm sure you'll enjoy it."

She squirms when I move lower, tracing her navel. "How long has she worked for you?"

"A couple of years." I drag a line from her navel to the apex of her sex, rolling my middle finger over her clit.

She sucks in a breath and presses her knees together. "I gave her a letter. She said you'll mail it for me."

"To your brother?" I trace her pussy lips with my thumb.

"Yes," she says, hardly suppressing a moan before biting her lip. "I wanted to tell you before Francine mentions it."

Ah, she was hoping to get her letter mailed without my knowledge but realized Francine will never undermine me. "You can write to Damian as much as you like."

She gives me a surprised look. "You don't mind?"

"Not in the slightest."

At the declaration, her body sags. I use the opportunity to part her slightly, playing just inside her opening without penetrating her with my finger. Her back arches. She moans. I slip a hand between her thighs and push them open wide, then urge her to settle back in my hold. She's so goddamn pretty spread over my lap with her nipples tight and arousal glistening on her pussy. Her breathing is shallower, her stomach rising and falling faster. I'm harder than before, painfully so, but I ignore the torturing feel of her ass on my cock, focusing only on her as I promised.

My play is soft and teasing, enough to stimulate but not enough to make her come. I won't take her pleasure unless we're fucking, unless I'm taking mine, or unless she asks me. I carry on with my stroking, extending the caresses to the inside of her thighs. She's trembling with full-blown shivers now.

Lowering my mouth to her ear, I press a kiss to the shell. "Do you want to come?"

"No," she says quickly, unwilling to surrender and admit defeat.

"It's no big deal." I tease her earlobe with my teeth. "We all need release. All you have to do is say yes."

She sighs, tilting her head to give me better access. I love how responsive she is to my touch, how I can coax her into the pleasure I want her to have. I love the smell of roses in her silky hair and the velvety petal smoothness of her skin. I love how wet and slick she is for me and how her ass lifts a little every time I rub a finger over her swollen clit. She's spread and on display, her lower body resting snuggly in my lap. Her eyes are closed and her head thrown back. She's a sight to behold. Since she's not saying no, I gather her wetness, careful not to overstretch her sensitive skin, and slip the tip of my finger into her heat. The hot tightness is torture. I can't help but imagine sinking my cock into her just like last night.

She gasps, her arms going rigid at her sides. It doesn't take long for her hips to follow my shallow thrusts. When her inner muscles go softer around my finger, I push in all the way to the knuckle.

Her thighs clench on my finger. "Maxime."

I lay her out like a sacrifice and bring my mouth down to kiss her nipple. I lick it lightly at first, then close my lips around the hard, little tip and lathe it with my tongue. She tastes delicious. I can't stop myself from French kissing her breast, covering her skin with sloppy kisses until her curve is wet. Her nipple hardens when I finally let go and cooler air washes over it.

Whimpering, she lifts her arms and rests them on her forehead.

"Do you want to come, Zoe?"

She keeps her eyes hidden from me, her expression sheltered under her arms. I feel her desire, how badly she wants to give in, but I won't take if she doesn't give it to me freely.

"Will it be bad if I say yes?" she asks in a small voice.

"No, Zoe. It won't be bad. Quite the contrary."

Her cry is defeated, a tremulous sigh. "Yes."

I increase the pace of my finger, pressing my thumb on her clit. She's so close, it only takes a few seconds before her body pulls as tight as a bow, her legs forming a V as the arrow hits right where I intended—in her soft little heart.

Women like Zoe feel the physical explosion of an orgasm on every level, most of all with their emotions.

She comes undone with a climax that locks her inner muscles around my finger and a tear that rolls over her cheek. It's victory and defeat, all rolled into one.

I withdraw slowly, taking care not to hurt her. Then I take her arms and arrange them around my neck where she most needs them to be, even if she doesn't know it herself. I hold her and give her something to hold onto as she comes back down to reality, to seeing herself naked in my arms like a shameful Eve saw herself for the first time before paradise turned into the garden of sin.

Grabbing the throw from the chair back, I cover her body, not only because the logs in the fire is burning out, but also because she'll feel vulnerable when the haze of passion dims. Reality is like winter, cold and unforgiving.

Her tears wet my neck, but she doesn't pull away. She burrows closer. I revel at the victory. There's nothing that can feel better, not my own release, not even the success of saving our business. The tenseness of my muscles is gone. The anger I felt when I entered this room has dissipated, vanished in the throes of her orgasm.

"There now." I kiss the top of her head. "It'll get better."

It's the vow I made to myself long before I made the promise to my father.

As we sit quietly in front of the last embers of the fire, Zoe dozes off. We didn't sleep much last night. The journey was tiring. I'm reluctant to wake her—I much prefer to stay like this with her in my arms —but it's dark outside. She has to eat.

I brush a strand of hair from her face and kiss her forehead. "Are you up for a shower?"

She yawns. "What time is it?"

I check my watch. "Almost six."

She stretches like a lazy cat. "I suppose."

My arms tighten around her involuntarily. She's cute, this little flower of mine. Balancing her in my arms, I stand to adjust my erection. I haven't forgotten about punishing her mouth. I've just moved it back to prioritize her needs. I unlock the door and carry her to my room. The hallway is lit, courtesy of Francine.

In the room, I switch on the light and turn up the heat before ordering Zoe to the bathroom.

She obeys wordlessly. The water in the shower comes on. I walk closer and put my ear to the door, listening to the sounds of cascading water, imagining her under the spray and wishing I could be there with her. Not yet. She's not ready for that.

A knock sounds on the door. I go over and open it. Fran stands on the step.

Her eyes dart toward the bathroom. "You've been away for less than a week."

"Meaning?"

"Meaning *that*," she points at the bathroom door, "was fast."

I swallow down my irritation. Fran is a loyal employee. "My private life isn't your concern."

"No?" She tilts her head. "It used to be."

"It's over, Fran. We've been through this."

Her eyes cloud over. "A couple of rolls between the sheets are enough to make you grow tired of a woman?"

Sadly, yes.

She motions with her head toward the bathroom. "How long do you think she'll last?"

"None of your business."

"She asked me to mail a letter."

"She told me."

"Why are the phones locked away, Max? Why isn't she allowed to leave the house?"

I clench my jaw. "As I said—"

"Not my business."

"Exactly."

She takes a step forward, putting our bodies flush. "I'm loyal to you." She snakes her arms around my neck. "You know that."

I grip her arms to pull them away. "But?"

"But I can't deal with having another woman flaunted—"

The bathroom door opens. We both turn our heads that way.

Zoe freezes on the threshold in a billow of steam. Clutching a towel to her chest, she looks between Fran and me. I don't like what I see in her expressive eyes. I don't like that wounded look or the sag of betrayal that sets in her shoulders.

I untangle Fran's arms and put her a step away from me.

Giving Zoe a cold look, Fran says, "Dinner is ready. I'll leave it in the warmer drawer before I go."

My voice is measured. "You do that."

With a last glance at me, Fran leaves.

"More than just your cook, I see." Zoe's chin is lifted but her eyes brim with emotions that spoil our earlier moment.

"It was a long time ago."

"Then you don't deny it. You fucked her."

I'm not going to lie. Not about that. "Yes."

"Thanks for that." She walks past me to the suitcase that lies unpacked on the bed. "I needed the reminder."

I catch her wrist. "You're not going to do this."

"Do what?"

"Look for excuses to shut me out."

"They're not excuses. They're facts, and why would I shut you out if you've never been inside to start with?"

I drop my voice an octave. "Careful, little flower. You don't know me. If you did, you wouldn't push me."

She yanks her arm free. "I know you better than you think."

It's a laughable generalization, a terrible misjudgment. Putting my hand on her shoulder, I push her down to her knees.

She fights it, straining back, and then fights the towel that threatens to fall open.

Unzipping my fly, I stare down at her shocked face. "I said we were going to punish that mouth. You owe me twice already." I pull out my cock, heavy and hard, thick with need. My balls ache with unspilled release.

She knows where I'm going with this when I stroke myself three times and aim for her lips. She clamps them shut. I grab her jaw and squeeze the pressure points next to her ears. It opens her mouth wide, wide enough to slide my cock through those plump lips. She gags and tries to pull back, but I grab the back of her head.

"You're going to take me," I hiss, "and swallow everything."

She grabs my thighs when I push her face forward, making her swallow my cock. Not caring so much about the towel now, it falls to the carpet, leaving her naked on her knees. Stunning. Struggling for air. I let her. She needs to learn this little lesson. Her very breaths belong to me. I can be kind or what she makes me out to be, either a cultured gentleman or the monster of her nightmares.

I count carefully, controlled. I'm in charge even as her saliva coats my dick and her tongue is warm on the underside, making me want to explode. I twist her locks around a fist and pull out when I get to ten. She gulps in air. Her big, blue eyes are watering, spit running down her chin. I'm being easy on her. She should be able to hold her breath to thirty without effort. I give her time for one more drag of air before I drive back. Then I move. I pump with two short thrusts and a long one, my cock hitting the back of her throat at every third count. I fuck her face on the beat of a waltz. It's a dance designed to limit her gag reflex and prevent her from vomiting.

My balls draw tight. Her lips are stretched thin around me, the noises she makes only spurring me on. I can last for a long time. Practice makes perfect. I can drag this out until she faints. I give her two more breathing reposes before I let myself go, aiming my cock deep and shooting my load down her throat. Her delicate white neck convulses as she tries to swallow with the intrusion in her throat. I spend every last drop, not sparing her before I pull out.

She sags in my hold, her chest heaving as her small body sucks in air. I don't let her go down. I keep her up by her hair. Using the long, silky tresses, I wipe my dick clean. Then I go down on my haunches, putting us on eye level.

Tilting back her head, I make her face me. "The choice, little flower, is always yours." I kiss her ravaged lips. "One punishment down. One to go."

Only then do I release her.

I go to the bathroom and shut the door. I need a shower. I strip and turn the water on the hottest setting I can handle. I let the burn scald me until fire rains over my skin.

I'm a depraved man.

I'll defile my little flower's body many times yet to come.

CHAPTER 15

Zoe

Hunched over, I catch my breath on the floor. My shoulders rise and fall rapidly with the air I try to suck in quietly, but I can't stop the loud panting completely. It's the sound of my humiliation. The warm tears blurring the pattern on the carpet is the sight and the carpet burns on my knees the feel. The taste is a lingering afterthought in my mouth. This is the portrait of degradation.

As oxygen feeds my lungs, the harshness of my breathing evens out. It turns from a perverse fight for air and dignity to searing anger that flares my nostrils and curls my shoulders outward like the edges of a piece of paper furling in a flame. Sitting back on my heels, I wipe the saliva from my chin. I still feel Maxime in the stretch of my lips and in the little tears in the corners. I still taste him on my tongue. The message was clear. My behavior has consequences. Play nice and be treated in kind.

My pride won't let me.

I want to hurt Maxime like he's hurting me. I want to insult him and crush him in every way I can, even as I give him my body. He just showed me he won't let me. He won't let me use him as a punching bag to gain the satisfaction of extracting some kind of revenge. He wants everything. He's not happy only with my body. He wants me to give it with a pretty please and a kind thank you. That's why he wants me to like the house and the food. He wants me to adapt, accept my fate, and give my body freely in return for his protection.

He'll make it as good for me as I make it for him.

Rationally, I know all of this, but my pride is a monster and my anger a dragon that live in my chest. They breathe fire into my soul until I'm blind to anything but the flames burning in my gut.

Fixing my gaze on the bathroom door, I push to my feet. I keep the target in sight as I move forward with balled hands and shoulders rolled inward. I grip the handle and fling the door open, stepping into the steam.

Maxime's body is a blurry image, an apparition in the fog through the glass. His back is turned to me, his head tipped back and big hands with bruised knuckles brushing over his skull. He's huge. His body dominates the space, but I don't miss a beat. I yank the shower door open.

He spins around, his gray eyes widening as he takes me in. Before the shocked expression on his face has vanished, I draw back my arm and slap him hard enough across the face to make his head fly sideways. Turning his face back to me, he touches his fingers to the imprint of mine on his cheek.

The fight leaves me with the outlet of violence. Just like that, the fire burns out. I've never been a physical fighter. I never wanted to be, not after my father, and shame and disappointment replace the anger, becoming the new monsters in my chest.

He doesn't give me a second to process what I'm becoming. Fast like the lash of a whip, he strikes out, grabbing my neck and arm and jerking me inside the shower. The breath leaves my lungs with an oomph as my back hits the tiles. Fear finds the front seat in my chest now as he stares at me with a clenched jaw and retribution burning in his eyes.

I expect him to hit me back. An ugly part of me wants him to so I can hate him more. Men like my father, those I understand, but Maxime is a complex mix of confusing signals. If my words made Maxime all but suffocate me with his cock, the mark I left on his skin should do much worse. I can't look away from his eyes. I watch their molten gray transform to a darker storm. With grinding teeth, he stares at me, his fingers tightening around my neck and pinning me against the wall. Just when I think he's going to snap my neck, he brings his head down and crushes our mouths together.

The kiss is brutal. His teeth cut my lip. I taste the blood as our tongues tangle. His breathing is harsh, his growl a primitive sound. He mashes our lips together, sucking the very life out of me as if this is a new kind of war. I fight back. I kiss him like my life depends on it. I don't know where my desperation comes from, only that this mutual roughness feels purging.

He takes, but I take, too. I bite down on his lower lip until our blood mingles. I use the aggression as an outlet for my pain like he won't allow me to use my sharp words or self-preserving pride. I stop being a passive participant, trying to hold onto something precious with both hands, something I don't want to share, and take something from him for myself.

It's a tipping point. To take, your hand has to be open, not clutched tightly around your heart. When I take from Maxime, I open myself. I'm vulnerable to the unknown, susceptible to the sensations of a violent kiss, surprised to find I like it. It's like a fight for life, a fight to death. Only one of us will be left standing when this is all over. The desperation transforms into arousal. Heat blooms between my legs. It's not gentle and slow building like in the study. It's instant and demanding. I moan, a keening sound of need that triggers Maxime's tipping point in turn.

He grows gentle. The warning hold on my neck loosens to a possessive caress. He drags his tongue over the cut on my lip and molds his mouth around mine with tender precision. It's a skilled kiss, a seductive kiss. I lean into it, pushing our bodies together. Placing one hand next to my face on the wall, he drags his hand from my neck to my breast, squeezing softly. My back arches. He tilts his hips toward mine, pressing his hard-on against my stomach. Water washes over us, drawing an abstract picture with blurry lines, but right and wrong vanishes with the need that pulses in my body as if it has a life of its own.

Like my aggression stoked his, his slower pace awakens new needs in me, a need to touch and to be held. Lifting my hands from the tiles where they're plastered next to my hips, I place them on Maxime's chest. The muscles are hard and unrelenting under my palms as I expected, but it's the bumpy texture of his skin that stills me.

I lean back, blinking the water from my eyes. Maxime freezes. His eyelids lift with wary apprehension. My gaze skims down. The skin of his chest is red and angry, patchy all the way to his stomach and covering half of his abdomen, an aggressive pattern of pain painted on a man. I've never seen anything like it. My heart squeezes in involuntary empathy. What happened to him? What caused such scars?

When I splay my fingers to inspect the damage, he catches my wrist.

The pressure of his grip is too hard. "Don't." The single word is harsh, but there's a plea in his eyes, and it's mixed with agony to reflect a portrait of stunning suffering in those ash-colored pools.

"What happened?" I whisper.

"Fire."

He moves my hand away, down, and places it over his erection. I close my fingers involuntary. He hisses. The sound gives me power. I stroke. He growls.

I know what he's doing. He's using distraction to prevent me from asking the questions turning in my mind, and it's working. His cock twitches under my palm, hardening more. I look at my fist, my fingers barely meeting, and back at his gaze.

He's watching me with sharp attention. I watch him in turn as I slide my fist up and down. I see what I do to him. I see the angry hunger in his eyes.

He cups my hip, angling his erection toward my opening. "Actions have consequences, little flower." He grabs my wrist and moves my hand away. "You came in here knowing full well what could happen."

I came in here to avenge myself for how he used me. Instead, I find myself pressed up against a wall, wet and needy. He grabs the base of his cock in one hand and presses the head against my clit while holding my hip with the other like I'm fragile and about to break. He rubs in a circle, sending flushes of heat through my body. Slickness covers my sex. He drags his cock over my opening, bringing my arousal back to my clit. I open my legs to give him better access. I'm panting, needing this now that I know what it feels like and how good the release is.

He rubs a thumb over my hip, a soft backward and forward brush. "I wasn't going to do this so soon."

When he grips my thigh and drapes it around his ass, I place my palms on his shoulders. I'm not going to let him make me forget why I came in here. There are lines he can't cross. "I won't let you bully me."

"Then stop bullying me."

His words take me by surprise. Is that how he sees my actions, my sharp tongue and spiteful attitude? I gasp, but not because of his words. He's parted me and slipped inside an inch. It burns, but not as much as last night.

"This isn't punishment," he says. "I don't want to hurt you. You can tell me to stop."

I don't. A spark ignites when he slides over sensitive nerve endings. Leaning my head against the tiles, I bite my lip, feeling the fire steal over my body, incinerating me from the inside out.

I adapt faster than yesterday. The stretch still hurts, but my body is suppler, welcoming the intrusion instead of trying to push it out. He's excruciatingly gentle, moving inch by inch until he is fully sheathed. He cups a hand between my legs, massaging my dark entrance with a middle finger. The stimulation makes me clench my knees together, trapping him inside me. My inner muscles squeeze. He curses and lets go, giving me room to relax and take him deeper.

I cling to his shoulders when he starts to move. His pace is slow and careful. He locks his hands around my middle, circling my waist. Bringing down his head, he catches my bottom lip between his teeth, sucking it gently into his mouth. He kisses me softly, reverently, as he drags his hands over my ribs to the sides of my breasts. He pushes the curves together between his palms until my nipples brushes over his chest. I feel the quick intake of his breath in our kiss. I hear it as he lets my breasts touch him where he wouldn't allow my hands.

His soft kiss and gentle touch stoke the fire inside me higher. Its fuel is as effective as the aggressive kiss that started this. Tilting my hips forward, I urge him to move faster and send me over the edge.

He's good at this dance. He knows the rhythm and the steps. He knows how to lead me. The way our bodies rub together stimulates my clit. I feel it coming, a band that stretches to breaking point.

"I'm going to—" The orgasm hits. It's white-hot and a symphony of pleasure exploding in every cell of my body. I dig my nails into his arms. A cry escapes my lips as he rips himself from me.

I want to mourn the premature ending of the fireworks under my skin, but when ribbons of cum erupt from his cock and fall over my thighs, I understand. I've almost forgotten a fundamental precaution. The consequences of him coming inside me make me go cold. Dammit. How could he disarm me this much? I haven't even asked if he's clean.

I'm scolding myself for my irresponsible behavior when he presses his forehead against mine. He's breathing heavily. We both are.

"Maxime."

He cups my cheek, this thumb hooking under my jaw. "What is it, Zoe?"

"We almost forgot."

He leans away to look at me. "I'm careful, but you're right. I'll take care of it first thing tomorrow."

"You're my first, but..." I bite my lip. I don't want to insult him again, not until I've decided how to move forward, if I'm willing to fight to the death of my soul or if I'm going to take the white flag he's offering.

His lips pull up in one corner. "Do you seriously think I'd risk giving you diseases?"

I study him. "I don't know." Despite what I said earlier, I don't really know him, and I'm having a tough time figuring him out. He's too confusing, a dangerous cocktail of mixed signals.

His mouth tightens. "I'm clean."

"Okay." It's a meek word, a feeble attempt at guarding our fragile peace.

"The water is getting cold."

He reaches for the sponge, soaps it, and starts to wash me. By the time he's done, the scalding hot water of earlier is lukewarm. He turns off the water and wraps me in a thick towel before taking one for himself. After drying me, he pulls on a T-shirt and a pair of tracksuit pants.

I'm lethargic and sore, and I have a strange glowing feeling in my body. I'm also hungry, and my stomach rumbles to announce it.

"Go to bed," he says, watching my reflection in the mirror as I'm brushing out my hair. "I'll bring up a tray."

I turn in surprise. "I can go down to eat."

"You're tired."

He doesn't wait for my response. He walks from the bathroom, leaving the door open. I go back to the room and rummage through the suitcase Maxime had packed, but there are no pajamas. He didn't get me any. I settle for a pair of silk panties, the ones that cover my bottom the most, and one of his T-shirts. Then I slip between the cold sheets, resting my back against the headboard.

I really am tired, and by the time he returns my eyes are drawing close.

He sits down next to me with a chuckle. "My little hellcat is exhausted."

I don't say anything. I'm not sure how I feel about what I did, about hitting him then kissing him like an animal and fucking as if we were having make-up sex. I don't want to turn into my father, my mother either.

He brushes a strand of hair behind my ear. "What's wrong?"

"Nothing." Except that I almost apologized to my kidnapper for slapping him. Am I losing my mind?

"Fran made *magret de canard*." He forks a bite-sized piece of meat and holds it to my lips.

I stiffen a little at the mention of his lover, or ex-lover as he's claimed, but I open my lips. I'm too hungry to refuse, hungrier than I've ever been. I'm surprised that I have an appetite at all. Maybe it's the sea air, or the colder winter, or the sex.

The duck is delicious. He alternates the meat with grilled potatoes, feeding me until the plate is empty.

"What about you?" I ask when he hands me a glass of red wine.

"I still have work to do. I'll eat later."

"Oh." I take a sip of wine, contemplating the man who fed me, taking care of my needs before his. Does he have a split personality? How can he be so caring in one moment and cruel in the next? Because he doesn't harbor feelings for me. I'm an object, his hostage.

He gathers the tray and stands. "It'll do you good to have an early night."

As if that will make everything all right.

"Goodnight, Zoe."

With that, he walks from the room. I stare at the closed door. I'm unsettled. Uncertain. It's only my first day in his house. How will I get through four years? I take another sip of the wine. It's good, rounded and smoky. It makes me feel warm and relaxed. What I need is some fresh air to clear my head. I need to decide how to handle this. I can't do this see-saw thing with Maxime. It's too exhausting. I'm either consenting to my fate or defying him to the point of my soul's destruction. What I can't do is become a person I hate. We'd vowed this to each other, Damian and I, that we'd never repeat our parents' mistakes.

I pull on a pair of socks and Maxime's thick robe that hangs behind the bathroom door. Taking my wine, I open the balcony doors and step outside. It's freezing. The wind nips at my skin, making me shiver. It's dark over the ocean save for the wedge of moonlight that illuminates the cove. A half-moon of sand shines in the light. There's a small beach at the bottom of the cliffs.

A movement on the boulder catches my eye. Someone is walking along the edge of the cliff. It's impossible not to recognize Maxime's powerful frame and purposeful stride. He's dressed in the same clothes from earlier, no coat. I suck in a breath. He'll catch his death out there.

I rest my arms on the rail, leaning over farther for a better view. He stretches his arms over his head. What the hell is he doing? He's taking off his T-shirt. Stunned, I watch as he strips naked. I'm caught so much off guard, I don't come to my senses until he steps right up to the edge and jumps.

CHAPTER 16

Maxime

The water is like icicles driving into my skin. The shock is thermal. It makes me feel alive. I go down deep, a place I've gone many times before, and not just literally. I don't swim. I don't fight. I let the cobalt hole swallow me, and I count. When I get to sixty, I start to kick. Another sixty, and I break the surface. Six times as much as I made Zoe take. If she suffered, I have to suffer too.

Gasping for air, I fight the cramps that set in due to the cold. My lungs burn. The punishment blazes through my chest like a fire while the cold encases my skin. I embrace it. Fuck, it feels great. Power surges through me. Strength bursts in my veins. I turn away from the shore and swim deeper into the ocean with strong breaststrokes. The cold vanishes until only the invincible sensation remains. In the stretch of moonlight that falls over the water, I float on my back to look at the stars. The sky is clear. It's a cold kind of clear, that dry, iciness that settles over the night and frosts the landscape like icing sugar sifted over a cake.

This is part of what I love so much about this place—the silence. I drift about aimlessly, enjoying the quiet and weightlessness for as long as I can. Chaos awaits on the shore. With a life like mine, there's always chaos. I should turn back soon. I may not feel the pain, but hypothermia will set in after a few more minutes. I drag my fingers over the scar tissue on my chest. The skin is dead. There's no feeling. There hasn't been since the multiple skin grafts.

That's the problem with men like me. We're unfeeling. It goes deeper than my scarred skin. It goes all the way down to the hardened, black, rotten organ I call my heart. In my occupation, we *do* things, *see* things. It desensitizes us. It makes us monsters to others and dead to ourselves. Until Zoe touched me.

When I held her against me in the lobby of her building, I felt something. It was different to the usual physical arousal that comes with sex. She stirred *things* inside me, things I thought were dead. She stirred my curiosity about life, about staying pure and beautiful amidst the sins that make grown men unfeeling. When she put her hands on my chest in the shower tonight, I swear my dead skin crawled. There was something there underneath the flesh and blood. I felt her touch in my heart. Longing. Compassion. Admiration. A need to protect. A need to please.

It's new. It's confusing. Fuck me if I know what to do with it.

What shall I do with her, my little flower? I look at the house that stands on the cliffs, a beacon of status and wealth with the lights shining from its windows. My gaze finds the room where she's sleeping, and then I still. A figure stands on the balcony, small and vulnerable against the evil myths and unfortunate truths that lurk in the night. A gust of wind rips her hair across her face. She shouldn't be out there. She'll catch pneumonia.

Turning back to the shore, I swim fast. I can find the passage between the sharp rocks blindfolded. In no time, I walk out on the sand, and when I look up, she's no longer there. I take the path, climbing up the steep steps to the cliff top where I left my clothes. I pull them on over my wet body and make my way back to the house.

I push the front door open, and Zoe stands there, hugging herself.

She's dressed in my robe, one of my T-shirts, and a pair of socks. A different kind of power surges through me. It has nothing to do with being invincible and everything about vulnerability. It's possessive. I'm overwhelmed with male pride, with owning what stands in front of me. My clothes mark her as mine. The way I took her body is an irrevocable claim. I'm jealous of her. I'm jealous of the men who'll have her when we're over, and suddenly the thought is unthinkable.

She's looking at me with parted lips, questions in her eyes. I lock away my revelations, the strangeness of these new feelings, and shut the door behind me.

Sleeking back my wet, windblown hair, I ask, "What are you doing up?"

"My God, Maxime." She steps toward me, her eyes big. "You'll freeze to death." She scans my face. "Your lips are blue."

Her concern warms my chest. Pathetically, I want more of her worry. "I thought you would've been glad if I dropped dead."

She grabs my arm and drags me deeper into the house. "Don't joke about that."

A smile plucks at my lips. It's not a forced gesture, but one of those spontaneous ones that feels so unfamiliar it must look unnatural. "About what? Death?" I'm not afraid of it. Not for myself. Yet for her I'm terrified.

She slaps my arm. "Shh. If you say it, you'll make it happen."

That makes me smile. It's not just a quirk of my lips. It's the full nine yards. "If I talk about my death, I'll die?"

Her blue eyes grow even rounder. "We attract what we think."

I'm intrigued. It's this part of her that fascinates me. "Do you believe in that hocus pocus hippy stuff?"

She gives me a chiding look. "It's not hippy stuff. It's quantum physics. It's the law of energy. What you give is what you get." Lifting a cocky brow, she continues, "You are what you think. Never heard about that?"

I cross my arms. "Is this a misguided lesson in morals?"

She scrunches up her nose. "No, it's science. For every action there's an equal reaction." She cocks her hip, her posture a challenge.

"You said so yourself, didn't you? Not in so many words, but if you think about it, we really believe in the same thing." She shrugs. "Actions have consequences."

She's cute, this tiny woman. I want to throw her over my shoulder and carry her away to somewhere nicer, someplace happier, but this is who we are, and we've already set the chain of actions in motion. It does give me insight into her mind and her thought process though, and I'm hungry to understand her.

I study her sassy little stance and saucy mouth. "It sounds as if you were thinking in my absence."

She clutches her hands behind her back. "I was."

I remain quiet, waiting for her to carry on, because I want to know how she operates. I want to know how she survives. Will she roll over and play dead, biding her time until it's up? Will she go into denial and pretend this isn't happening by living out some bullshit fantasy in her mind? Will she surrender? Or will she fight me until the end? What makes her tick? What will her strategy be in our war?

She blushes a little. "I'm not going to give you any more trouble."

I'm guessing the color in her cheeks is due to shame and not shyness. It's the knock she takes in willingly being the lesser, submitting to a fate she'd otherwise never have chosen. But her shoulders are square, and her head is high. This isn't surrender. She's either playing dead or fighting the only way she can, by choosing her battles wisely.

Uncrossing my arms, I move closer. "Is that what you were doing outside on the balcony? Making important decisions?"

She takes a step back. "You saw me?"

"You should've dressed warmer. The wind is cold."

"You're one to talk. I saw you jumping off that cliff in nothing but your birthday suit."

"Is your concern for the cold, the jump, or the fact that I was naked?"

"None." She backtracks when I advance another step. "I'm not concerned about you."

"No? Then why do you behave like you are?"

"The only thing I'm concerned about is what happens to me if you die."

Ah. That sours my mood a little, not that I could've expected differently. "Right. You should be since I have your passport, not to mention that you'll be given to Alexis."

The pink disappears from her cheeks.

"You don't have to worry your pretty little mind over things like that. I'm not planning on dying soon, and I'm glad we can put the fights aside." I cup her cheek. I'm going to figure her out, this clever little daisy. "I meant what I said. You can be happy here."

She nods. "Okay."

"What made you change your mind?" Jokingly, I add, "Seeing me jump off a cliff?" Had I known it would be this easy, I'd have done it sooner.

She looks away. "The way I behaved reminded me too much of my father."

Gripping her chin, I turn her face back to me. "The way you behaved how?"

She averts her eyes. "When I slapped you."

I don't like where this is going. "What did your father do, Zoe?"

"He was violent."

My back goes rigid. "With you?"

"Mostly with my mother and Damian, but he broke things, and it scared me."

I try to picture Zoe as a child, a little girl, scared and defenseless, and I don't like it. I don't fucking like it one bit. I admire her for fighting her genes, for wanting to be better. I sure as hell didn't manage.

"I see." I drop my hand. "Do I remind you of your father?"

She lifts her gaze back to mine. "No." Just as my spine relaxes, a sliver of fear creeps into her tone. "You're in a different league. My father wasn't a tenth of what you are."

She fears me more. I both hate and love it. I can't decide which feeling I want to embrace. Just when I thought I almost had her figured out she confuses me again. Confused isn't something I've ever been. I don't like it.

Staring at her big, frightened eyes, I move even closer, my body shadowing hers. I want her. I want her fear and pleasure. I want her happiness and submission. I want to take her right here on the stairs. I barely manage to grit out, "Go to bed."

She doesn't let me tell her twice. She runs up the stairs like a mouse fleeing from a cat. I stand at the bottom, staring after her while mulling over her words and dissecting my feelings. Making sense of thoughts and sensations is a logical process. I don't trust my heart. I only trust my mind.

I suppose what she said about being worse than her father is true. I've broken a lot more than material things. There's more blood on my soul than on the hands of a soldier. I suppose I do scare children, and puppies, and pretty little innocent flowers, but I'm neither coward nor fool. Her father was a coward for terrorizing his own daughter and a fool for not seeing the pure, perfect girl right under his eyes.

An insight hits me. Zoe grew up with violence. However wrong that is, she should be used to it, at least to an extent. What I am should scare her, but it shouldn't surprise her. She shouldn't be as innocent as she is. She avoided reality. The only means she had of escaping a traumatic childhood was hiding in herself by going someplace else in her head. That's why Zoe is a dreamer. That's why she's a romantic. Her reality was a shithole, but she desperately held out for cupids and happily-ever-after. That's why she's a princess, down to the way she dresses.

Warfare is an art. It requires a certain finesse. There's little finesse in slaying your enemy by cutting off his head. It's much more challenging to turn him into an ally. It's much more rewarding to have your enemy worship at your feet. This new insight tells me exactly what my strategy with Zoe should be. I'm not going to be her father. I won't allow her to live in her head where she can hide from me. In the art of warfare, it's crucial to know your enemy's vulnerability. Now that I know hers, I'll fill that gap. I'll give her what she most wants.

Before her time here is up, she'll be eating out of my hand. When the time comes to set her free, she'll beg me to stay. Yes, I like this outcome much better than keeping her chained with threats. My chest heats just thinking about it. My cock hardens at the challenge.

My own daisy, in a vase on my table. I didn't steal it from someone's garden. It was growing wild on the pavement, right there for the taking.

CHAPTER 17

Zoe

Persistent shaking pulls me from my sleep. I fight it, but I can't ignore the deep voice or the French accent. I wake with a gasp when I remember where I am.

"Easy, Zoe." Maxime brushes a hand over my shoulder. "You have to wake up. We have an appointment in Marseille."

Rubbing my eyes, I turn to face him. He sits on the edge of the bed, dressed in a dark suit. His hair is still damp from his shower. The smell of winter hangs like a faint cloud around him, but it's pierced with the summery fragrance of roses. A cup of steaming tea stands on the nightstand.

"I brought you an infusion," he says. "Fran can make you coffee if you prefer. Breakfast is waiting downstairs."

"Thank you," I say uncertainly, my manners still intact while I'm half asleep.

"You're welcome." He takes my hand and kisses the back, then puts something in my palm.

I lift my hand and stare at the cellphone.

"My number is programmed." He gets to his feet. "Come down when you're ready. We're leaving in thirty minutes."

I only get to my senses when he's gone. Maxime had opened the curtains. The sky outside is still dark, dawn barely breaking through a thick layer of clouds. I look at the telephone screen again. The time says it's eight o'clock.

Wait. I have a phone.

Shooting upright, I type in the number for the correctional service where Damian is held and press dial. A message comes on in English, announcing I don't have access to the service. I check the settings. Of course. I can only dial Maxime's number. I didn't expect anything different, but my shoulders sag in disappointment.

Dejected, I reach for the tea on the nightstand. Folding my hands around the cup, I inhale the fragrant herbal tea. It smells of roses and raspberries, the same tea Maxime served me in Venice. I take a sip. It's a delicious blend. The brew warms and somewhat fortifies me.

Memories of last night's discussion turn in my head as I shower and change into a pair of slacks and a cashmere sweater with frilly sleeves that have been neatly arranged in the dressing room. Maxime must've unpacked the suitcase either last night or this morning. I thankfully fell asleep before he came to bed. I wasn't going to unpack. Putting the clothes he'd bought for me in his closet doesn't only feel wrong, but also way too final. After putting on a pair of ankle boots, I go downstairs where a breakfast of croissants and orange juice is set out in the dining room. Maxime is seated at the table, reading something on his phone. Judging by the pastry flakes in his plate, he's already eaten.

When I enter, he gets up and pulls out a chair for me.

"Sleep well?" he asks.

"Yes." Surprisingly. "Why are we going to Marseille?"

"You have a doctor's appointment."

Of course. Relief flows through me. The last thing I want is an unplanned pregnancy.

He checks his watch. "I have a few instructions to give to Fran before we leave. Any meal preferences for this week's menu?"

I shake my head. I don't care what I eat. I hate that I have to eat Maxime's food at all.

"Maybe later," he says with a stiff smile.

I eat quickly, and when he returns, I'm ready.

Like yesterday, Maxime drives us while two men follow in their own car. I stare at the scenery outside, at the cliffs, the beach, and the city that comes into view forty minutes later. From afar, the buildings aren't impressive. The only piece of architecture that stands out is the church on the top of the hill. As we enter the center of town, the buildings change from white concrete blocks to beautiful old ones with French windows, blue shutters, and ornate balcony rails. He parks in front of a building with a sculptured entrance, each top corner supported on a marble angel's shoulders.

"Wow," I say as I look up at the carved wooden door.

Putting a hand on my back, he buzzes us in and leads me up a stone staircase to the third floor. A middle-aged man with mousy hair and glasses opens the door when Maxime rings.

"Max." He pats Max on the back before extending a hand toward me. "Mademoiselle Hart. I'm Dr. Olivier."

I accept the handshake automatically. From the fact that he speaks English, Maxime must've briefed him about me before we arrived. What did he tell the doctor? That I'm his willing lover? Or does the doctor know the truth?

"Come through," the doctor says, showing us into an examination room.

The far end next to the fireplace serves as a sitting area. Maxime takes my hand and leads me to the sofa. He pulls me down next to him, not letting go of my hand but arranging it on his thigh instead. It's an intimate act, a loving one almost, and the doctor's gaze slips to our intertwined fingers as he takes the chair. It's acting, all part of the role Maxime plays. That means the doctor doesn't know the circumstances of why I'm here.

"So." The doctor adjusts his glasses and gives me a curious look. "You're here for birth control."

My cheeks heat at the implication. My fingers involuntarily clench on Maxime's thigh. He rubs a thumb over my knuckles in a soothing gesture as he replies, "We want what's least invasive for Zoe."

"The injection is very efficient with minimal hormonal side effects. It also eliminates the possibility of forgetting to take the pill, which makes it more effective."

"The shot, then," Maxime says.

"I've prepared everything." Dr. Oliver clears his throat. "Do you have any questions, Zoe?"

I glance at Maxime.

"Go on," he says with a smile. It's a practiced smile, one he puts up for show.

"How long before it's safe?" I ask.

"Seven days," the doctor replies, "so use additional protection for the next week or two." He stands. "You can sit over there in the examination chair."

While the doctor prepares the shot, Maxime takes me to the chair and rubs a finger over my pulse.

"This won't hurt," Dr. Oliver says, approaching with a hypodermic needle.

I've never liked needles or blood. I get queasy at the sight of both, so I turn my head away while he works. It doesn't hurt much, just a small prick, but I jump nevertheless when he inserts the needle.

Maxime brushes a strand of hair from my forehead. "Does it hurt?"

"No," I say. "I'm just not good with sharp things being stabbed into my skin."

Maxime's smile is genuine this time—amused—and the usual frost in his eyes a few degrees warmer. "Do you have a low pain threshold?"

I narrow my eyes. "Are you making fun of me?"

"Never," he says, but his smile doesn't fade.

A short while later, the doctor has also taken a blood sample. Maxime thanks Dr. Olivier and writes out a check. They shake hands, and we're on our way.

In the car, Maxime takes my hand as he steers the automatic into the traffic. "You look pale."

"It's the blood. It makes me feel like fainting."

He squeezes my fingers. "You need a hearty lunch. Have you tried *bouillabaisse?*"

"No."

"It's a local specialty. I'll take you to a place. I just have to take care of some business first."

We drive through the old town to the hilly part until we're on the outskirts of town. A property twice the size of Maxime's comes into view. The mansion is built in the same style with wooden shutters and a balcony that runs around the first floor.

"This is my parents' place," he says. "You'll wait here."

I sit up straighter. "With your mother?"

He glances at me. "Is that a problem?"

"She doesn't like me." It was clear in every part of her body language.

He presses a button on an intercom at the gate. "My mother is old-fashioned. She doesn't believe in sex before marriage."

"Then she won't want me here," I say as he pulls up to the house and parks in a circular driveway.

He pats my hand that still rests on his thigh. "She'll get used to the idea."

I doubt that very much, but he's already coming around to get my door. Taking my hand, he pulls me toward the main entrance. The wind is freezing. It penetrates my very bones. A woman in a maid's uniform opens the door. She's young and pretty with chestnut hair.

Maxime greets her in French and exchanges a few words while she takes our coats before leading me through the lobby to a sitting room that overlooks the garden.

"We're lucky," he says. "Maman is having a friend over for tea."

I pull back. "I hate to impose."

He stops to look down at me. "You're with me, Zoe. That makes you a guest. Guests don't impose."

I'm not sure what to say to that, but before I can find my words, we enter the lounge where Cecile Belshaw sits with another woman. The remnants of a tea party are spread out on the coffee table. In the middle of the teacups and saucers stands a pink mousse cake with a couple of slices missing.

"Max?" Cecile's tone is friendly, but her eyes tighten as she puts down her teacup.

She says something in French. The other woman, who's around the same age as Cecile, looks between Maxime and me. I don't know what they're saying or if it's about me, but her spine stiffens as she takes me in. Her smile is so fake it looks painted on her face. Cecile addresses her son in a pleasant voice that's no less fake.

Maxime switches to English. "This is my aunt, Hadrienne. She's my mother's sister-in-law." He bends down and kisses her cheeks. "How are you, Hadrienne? This is Zoe."

She nods and says with a heavy accent, "How do you do?"

"Pleased to meet you." What else can I say?

"I'll be back before lunch." Maxime kisses my forehead and then turns to his mother. "Take good care of her."

I watch his back as he strides away. The door shuts behind him with a click. Silence prevails. I turn back at the two women who are looking at me as if I'm garbage that blew in from the street.

Cecile sighs. "You better sit, Zoe."

The only free space is the seat next to Hadrienne, unless I'm to take one of the chairs standing on the other side of the room. She scoots up when I sit, putting as much distance between us as the couch allows.

"Tea?" Cecile asks in an icy tone.

A drink to warm me up will be welcome, but that's not why I accept. I agree because I need something to do with my hands. If not, I'll fidget. "I'll get it."

She gives me a startled look. "I'll remind you this is my house."

"Oh, I didn't mean to be rude. I only wanted to save you the trouble."

"I can pour my tea in my home, thank you very much." She exchanges a look with Hadrienne. "Foreign customs."

Hadrienne raises a brow.

I let Cecile pour my tea, and thank her as I take the cup, but decline a slice of cake.

An uncomfortable silence falls over the room again.

"Where were we?" Cecile asks after a few beats. "Oh, yes. We were talking about gooseberry tart for dessert on Sunday. It's so complicated to think and speak in English."

Fine. I understand her irritation. I'm an uninvited guest, disrupting their tea party, but does she have to be so rude? I'm not Maxime's girlfriend. I owe them nothing. I don't have to take this.

"You don't have to speak English on my behalf." I wave a hand. "Just carry on in French. Your chatter will most probably bore me, anyway."

Cecile's cheeks light up, two red apples on a pale background. "I beg your pardon?"

Leaving the cup on the table, I stand. "I'll have a walk in the garden, if you don't mind. It's stopped raining, and I can do with some exercise."

Hadrienne laughs. "Oh, do sit down, girl." To Cecile she says, "You have to admit, she's got some backbone."

Cecile clenches her jaw. "Maybe you should have some cake, Zoe. I think eating is a better occupation for your mouth than speaking."

My lips part. I'm about to tell her to go to hell, but Hadrienne grabs my wrist and pulls me back down. "Enough of that. It's a long time to lunch. I'm sure we can find something neutral to talk about."

"What is your problem?" I ask Cecile.

"Me?" She makes big eyes. "You're imagining problems where there are none."

Right.

"There now." Hadrienne smoothes out her skirt. "Why not tell us how you met."

"In South Africa," Cecile says. "A speedy romance. Then again, money makes everything go faster, doesn't it?"

"You think I'm after Maxime's money?" I ask.

Raising a pinky, Cecile lifts the cup to her lips. "I never said you're after his money."

"You implied it." I move to the edge of my seat. "That's the same thing."

Cecile rolls her eyes. "Oh, it's not. Don't overreact."

I don't care what Maxime's reaction will be. I can't just sit here any longer. Pushing to my feet, I say, "Excuse me. If I stay, I'm afraid I'll say something disrespectful."

"You know what's disrespectful?" Cecile puts down her cup. "Coming here and attacking me in my own house."

"Attacking you?" I ball my hands. "Do you really expect me to keep quiet and accept your insults?"

"Yes," she says evenly. "I expect you to shut up. That's the least you can do."

What's wrong with these people? Turning on my heel, I walk to the French doors and push them open. Escaping outside, I walk down a path that leads to a gazebo at the end of the garden. At the edge, I stop to breathe in the salty air and let the small freedom fill my lungs.

I hate them. I hate them all. I wish I could run. I wish I could climb down the steps to the street at the back and sneak onto a train and go wherever it takes me. I don't care that I don't have a passport or money. I can work. I can always make a plan. What I can't do is let Damian get hurt.

My fingers curling into fists, I take in the view of this strange and unwelcome place.

Four years. Give or take a few, to quote Maxime's words.

I feel like screaming. I feel like hurling the bird feeder that hangs from the branch of a pine tree into the street, but that won't help me one bit. I can't let Cecile get to me. I don't care what she thinks. Why should I care about how she treats me?

I settle on the bench in the gazebo, staring out at the sea. Why did Maxime even help me? He didn't have to. He could've just left me to my fate. I don't understand his motives. I'm not even sure it's about sex. He said he's had many lovers. Francine seemed quite willing.

"Well, look who's here," a male voice says behind me.

I jump.

Alexis comes around the bench with my coat in his hand. "I didn't mean to scare you." Holding out the coat, he says, "You forgot this."

Thinking of the devil. When I reach for the coat, he holds it open like a gentleman, instead. Warily, I get up so he can help me slip into it. His hands rest on my shoulders for a second before he sets me free. I step away and turn back to face him. He's handsome in the blond hair and fair skin kind of way. The color of his eyes leans more toward blue than his brother's. Recalling what Maxime had said about him, a shiver runs over my body.

Watching me with his head tipped down, he asks, "How are things with my brother?"

I fold one side of the coat over the other. "Why don't you ask him yourself?"

He smiles. "Touché. Is he treating you all right?"

"What do you care?"

"I don't know what my brother told you, but I'm not your enemy, Zoe."

"No?" I look him over. "Then what are you? My *friend*?"

"There's no need to say it like that."

My fingers tighten on the fabric I clutch to my chest. "How would you like me to say it? My kidnappers? My jail keepers?"

He holds up a hand. "Maybe friends isn't the right term, but no one wants it to be bad here for you. We're not monsters, you know."

His expression and words are so sincere I have a hard time processing them.

"That's why I asked how Max is treating you," he continues.

"You're concerned?" I ask mockingly. "You expect me to believe that?"

He taps his temple. "Max isn't always right up here. Ever since the accident..."

My heart starts beating faster. "What accident?"

"The fire. Didn't he tell you?"

I shift my weight, eyeing the distance to the gazebo steps. I feel like a bird trapped by a cat. "He mentioned it."

"Arson. Someone set fire to one of our warehouses. Max was trapped inside." He rubs his forehead. "No one should've been able to survive those flames. The pain must've been excruciating. After Max walked out of there, he never was quite the same."

I shudder at the mental picture. "Are you saying he's insane?"

"What I'm saying," Alexis says, "is that you have to be careful."

"Talking about me?" a deep, familiar voice asks.

I spin around to see Maxime approaching with a dark look on his face.

"We were just getting acquainted," Alexis says with a cold smile.

Maxime steps up next to me. "You don't speak to her when I'm not around."

"That'll be a tad difficult," Alexis says, "seeing that she's part of your household now and our paths are sure to cross more often than not. You can't always be everywhere, can you?"

Maxime grabs my arm. "It's time to go."

Alexis salutes. "I'm looking forward to seeing you on Sunday, Zoe."

"She's not going," Maxime bites out.

Alexis pulls his face into a shocked expression. "You're leaving her all by herself in that stuffy old house while we're having a party? How rude of you, brother. Don't worry, Zoe. I'm happy to keep you company. My social skills are not as unpolished as my brother's."

Maxime puts his face in Alexis's. "You don't want to test me."

"Having authority issues, Max?"

Maxime's hold on my arm turns painful. His other hand clenches at his side. "I dare you, little brother." His smile is thin and cruel. "I'd love a reason to give you the treatment you deserve."

Maxime pulls me roughly down the steps and onto the path, walking with such long strides I'm battling to keep up. Cecile and Hadrienne get up when we enter the lounge.

"Max." Worry is etched on Cecile's face. "What happened?"

"Nothing." He kisses his mother's cheeks. "See you on Sunday."

He all but drags me to the car and shoves me inside. When he comes around and takes the wheel, I try to make myself small against the door. My heart is still thumping in my chest. I can't stop thinking about what Alexis said. There's not much love lost between the brothers. There's no question that they're both manipulating me, but which one is telling the truth?

CHAPTER 18

Maxime

Alexis loves fucking with me, but I won't let him fuck with Zoe. She doesn't know this family and their layers of nuances. She has no way of protecting herself against the mind games we play. It'll take her years to figure us all out.

I glance at her as I change the gears. "No more talking to Alexis."

She gives me an incredulous look. "What am I supposed to do when he talks to me? Ignore him? Pretend I don't hear?"

"Just say I don't want you to talk to him." Possessiveness is something every man in this family understands.

She shrugs. "Fine."

"What did he say to you?"

"That you're insane."

I laugh. "He's probably right."

She gapes at me. "You're not upset?"

"I don't get upset about things that don't matter."

She looks back at the road. "Wait. Why are we heading home? I thought you wanted to eat in town."

"I changed my mind."

"Just like that."

"Yeah. Just like that."

"I see."

"No, Zoe. You don't."

"What's that supposed to mean?"

I pull over at the outlook point and park. "Get out."

Her eyes grow large. "What?"

"Get out of the car."

"You're leaving me here?"

"Did I say I was leaving you here?"

She looks around the unbuilt area, and then up the deserted road. No doubt escape is at the forefront of her mind. It probably will be for a while still to come. She'll dream about it like recovered addicts dream about drugs and ex-smokers dream about cigarettes. A turning point will come when her dreams will evolve around staying and building a nest for herself.

Giving me an uncertain glance, she grips the handle and opens the door. She steps into the somber day, her hair blowing in every direction.

I shut down the engine and get out. "Walk to the edge."

She turns her face toward the cliff. When she looks back at me, her face is pale with fear. "Are you going to make me jump?"

"No." I move around the car, closer to her. "Go."

She gives me a pleading look. "I don't want to."

"Go, Zoe." She needs to learn to trust me, even when she's frightened.

She walks to the edge, carefully peering down. A frown mars her features. "What is that?"

"What does it look like?"

"A picnic?"

I take her hand. "Come. There's a path this way."

She pulls free. Her voice is angry. "You scared me. You could've just told me why we stopped here."

"Then it wouldn't have been a surprise."

"I thought…"

"I was going to kill you?"

"Yes," she whispers.

"I've told you before. I'm not going to kill you."

"How do I know you won't change your mind?"

"You don't."

Her chest rises with a deep breath. "Is this one of your lessons?"

"Yes."

Her beautiful eyes are filled with apprehension. "What am I supposed to learn from this?"

"To do something when I tell you to."

She scoffs. "Blind obedience?"

"As long as you do as you're told, I'll watch out for you." I take back her hand. "Now come."

We climb down the path to the small beach below. It's private, part of our territory. I was going to take her for the best bouillabaisse in town until I called to make a reservation and found out my uncle and father were lunching there. The picnic is improvised, a stab at fulfilling her romantic needs, but right now there's nothing romantic about the way I feel. Volatile is more like it.

When we reach the beach, Zoe pulls her hand free and walks to the edge of the water. She stares out over the ocean, a small, lonely, sad figure, and something stirs in my chest. I pop the cork of the champagne and pour her a glass.

"Come here," I say.

She turns away from the water and sits down on the blanket. I hand her the champagne, and then prepare a plate of cheese, charcuterie, and baguette.

"Hungry?" I ask as I put the plate between us.

"A little."

"Eat up."

I let her eat and drink, filling her glass twice while only having one myself. I'm driving, but that's not why I'm pumping her full of champagne. I'm getting her drunk. I need her uninhibited.

"That's enough for me," she says when I offer her another piece of Brie.

Setting the food aside, I push her down.

"What are you doing, Maxime?"

I straddle her legs. "Having my dessert."

"Here?" she cries out.

"Wherever I want."

"What if someone—"

Her words cut off when I push up her coat and unfasten her pants. I pull them down her hips with her underwear and flip her around.

There's a tremor in her voice. "Maxime."

I wrap my arm around her waist and pull her to her knees. She looks at me from over her shoulder, her pretty face tense, but it's only until I bury my fingers in the tight flesh of her globes and drag my tongue over her pussy. The frown on her brow evens out as she pinches her eyes shut. I repeat the action, this time spearing my tongue through her folds. Her lips part. The tension in her pretty features turns to desire. She's not complaining about the location any longer. All thoughts of our unsuitable spot have vanished from her mind, courtesy of a small dose of lust and three glasses of expensive French champagne.

She moans when I sink my tongue deeper. I don't waste time. I suck her clit and work a finger inside her wet heat, getting harder as I remember exactly how tightly her inexperienced pussy grips my cock. She comes with a cry, her back arching and her fingers burying in the blanket.

My pants are unzipped and my cock free before her orgasm is over. I take a condom from my pocket and make quick work of sheathing my cock. She's wet. She's ready. Gripping her hips, I push in carefully. Her moans are loud. She's tight and warm, gripping me like a fist. I can go harder on her because of the alcohol. Her body is supple and relaxed. She pushes back, taking me deeper, and I slam all the way home. Her cry makes me even harder. It makes me take her with punishing strokes. Twisting her long hair around a fist, I use it like a rein, pulling her head up and to the side until she faces me. I want to see the ecstasy on her face as I fuck her into oblivion.

I'm rough, but she arches her back and makes sexy, needy little sounds. I fuck her until her arms give out and she goes down on her elbows, until pleasure erupts at the base of my groin and fills up the condom instead of her body. One day, I'll empty myself inside her. I'll mark her. When I do, no man will ever touch her again. She'll belong to me forever, not only for four years.

I ease her down gently and cover her body with mine, making sure to keep my weight on my elbows.

Pressing a kiss behind her ear, I say, "No more talking to Alexis."

She turns her head to the side, her cheek flat on the blanket and her breathing heavy. "Is that what this is about? That's what you're trying to teach me? That you'll fuck me like it's a punishment in broad daylight where anyone can see if I speak to your brother?"

I pull out, causing her to whimper. The beach is secluded. You can't see it unless you look over the cliff, and the boats don't sail past this cove. There are too many rocks in the shallow water. I wasn't planning on doing this, either, when I set up the picnic. Fucking her here became a part of my intentions after I caught her with Alexis. Yes, I want her to accept me inside her body anywhere and anytime, and yes, I don't want her to talk to Alexis, but that's not what this is about.

She's mine. All mine.

That's the lesson.

CHAPTER 19

Zoe

It must be the effect of the champagne, but it's after nine when I wake up the next morning. The cup of rose tea on the nightstand is cold. Maxime's side of the bed is empty. He must've gone to work.

After showering and changing, I use the same stationary to write another letter to Damian. Emails aren't allowed, although he has limited access to a computer for the studies he took up in jail.

I seal the letter in an envelope and go downstairs. A breakfast of croissants and oranges are laid out on the dining room table. I eat quickly, then carry my plate to the kitchen. Francine is standing at an island counter, chopping onions. She's dressed in black pants and a silk blouse with a white apron tied around her waist. She lifts her eyes when I enter but doesn't say anything.

I put the plate in the dishwasher and lean against the counter. "I have another letter. If you tell me where to leave it—"

"In the silver tray in the entrance."

"Look, I…" I get why she doesn't want me here, but I can't tell her I don't have a choice. I remember Maxime's threat all too well, and he's a man of his word. That's another lesson he's taught me.

"I'm busy," she says. "I'm here to cook, not to chitchat when you're bored."

"Does Maxime read the letters?"

She gives me an irritated look. "I'm not psychic. You'll have to ask him."

Fine. This is how she's going to play it. I straighten and walk to the door.

Her words stop me in the frame. "You won't last, Zoe."

My name is like an insult on her lips. I look back at her from over my shoulder. "It seems you didn't."

Her cheeks flush red. "I'm here, am I not?" She smiles. "We'll see where you are when he grows tired of you."

A rather frightening thought. I hope not on the bottom of the ocean.

FOR THE REST of the day, I install myself in front of the fire in the library. I page through the coffee table books with photos of the region, but I can't focus. I switch on the television and figure out how to set the language to English. I've never owned a television, and I lose myself in a spy series, but by late afternoon I'm hungry and bored. I've skipped lunch.

Pushing the throw aside, I go in search of something to eat in the kitchen and find a salad and a glass of water set on the table in the dining room. I eat listlessly before washing my plate and glass in the kitchen. Francine has already left. A casserole stands on the stove.

I walk to the window and peer out. It's rainy today. Drops lash at the windows. The ocean is obscured in a haze of fog. The grounds that stretch to the edge of the cliff are green with hedges and bushes trimmed into shapes. A maze stands in the middle.

I go from window to window, looking at the garden from different angles. I arrange the books in the library in alphabetical order. I switch the television on and off. Finally, I sit down in my favorite chair in front of the fireplace and stare at the flames. Normally, I would've daydreamed to pass the time, but dreaming isn't my go-to escape any longer. That dream, the one about Venice and love, has been vandalized. It hurts too much to poke at it or to try and construct something new from the debris that's left.

It's dark when the front door opens. The fire has long since burnt out. A light flicks on in the entrance. Heavy footsteps approach. I turn my head toward the sound. Maxime stops in the frame.

"What are you doing in the dark?" he asks.

"I haven't noticed."

He flicks on the light. He's wearing a black suit and purple shirt. "That you can't see your hand in front of your face?"

"I was looking at the fire."

He glances at the ashes, and then at the photo book on the coffee table. "What did you do with yourself today?"

"I arranged the books alphabetically." A belated thought strikes me. "I hope you don't mind?"

He looks at the shelves. "You didn't strike me as the OCD type."

I shrug.

His steps are purposeful as he walks over and stops in front of the chair. "Come here."

I made a promise. I said I wouldn't give him trouble. Slowly, I rise.

Approval sparks in his gray eyes. "Take off my tie."

Reaching up, I untie the knot and pull the tie from his collar.

His face is harsh, his features always frightening, but there's something friendly, playful almost, in his expression when he says, "Go pour me a drink."

My first reaction is resistance. It's like telling a dog to fetch a newspaper. I'm not his damn servant. Yet yesterday's lesson with the picnic gives me pause. Fine. I'll trust him on this. I'll play along.

I go to the wet bar and pour a few fingers of whiskey the way I saw him do it, then carry the glass back to him. Our fingers brush when he takes it.

"Thank you," he says, holding my gaze as he takes a sip.

The way he looks at me heats my belly. It's a stare that communicates want, need, shared secrets, and praise. It's the praise that makes the warmth spread to my chest. I've always been a pleaser.

His lips curve as he hands me the glass. It's more than offering to share his drink. It's sharing a private moment and a part of himself with me. He's opening up, letting me in. He's making himself vulnerable. That's what this lesson is. He didn't order me to fetch his drink to humiliate me. He's showing me how to be kind to him, and how my kindness will be rewarded in return.

I turn the glass and put my lips on the spot where his has been. His eyes widen a fraction, surprise thawing their usual coldness. The alcohol burns down my throat when I swallow. Taking the glass back from me, he leaves it on the table and reaches for the zipper of my dress. Without the fire it's cold, but I let him push the dress over my shoulders and hips. My breasts tighten in the lace cups of my bra. The matching panties grow wet. Now that I've had a taste of the forbidden, my body craves it.

He drags his gaze over me, lingering on the underwear and long boots. "I think I'll leave those on."

The approval of earlier turns into a different kind of approval, something more carnal than appraisal. He likes what he sees, and he doesn't mind making himself vulnerable by showing me. No. He's exposing himself on purpose, rewarding my trust by giving me power. The exchange feeds the part inside me that needs approval and above all kindness. I'm starving for this kindness. I *need* this kindness.

As he shrugs out of his jacket and starts unbuttoning his shirt, a revelation hits me. This is nothing but science, the law of energy. The more he tortures me, the more I need kindness to restore the imbalance in my soul. What he proved yesterday when he forbade me to speak to his brother is that the only person permitted to give me kindness is Maxime himself. The man who torments me is the only man who can make it better.

The cure for my pain is the cause of the pain.

It's confusing. It feels like a mind-fuck. It's messing with my head as he unbuckles his belt and pulls down his zipper. I need distance from this, to figure out what he's doing to me, but his cock is hard and huge. I know it'll hurt a bit, and I need that, too. Maybe it's to punish myself for giving in to the emotional needs I allow him to fulfill. Maybe I'm flogging myself with physical pain for my weakness.

He removes his shoes and socks and straightens to stand naked in front of me. He shows me his scars and ugliness, a gift for my kindness. He's exposed—vulnerable—but so am I, and I can't tell the difference between manipulation and lessons any longer. Not that it matters, because when he touches me, my mind recedes to a place where thoughts don't matter. All that matters is the burning desire for him to hurt and please me, to bring me relief from the torment he orchestrates with such clever design in both my body and soul.

He steps up against me, letting his cock brush my stomach. "Don't think so hard, my little flower."

No, he wouldn't want me to think, because thinking leads to the truth. "What do you want me to do?"

His voice is husky, a foreign accent targeted on seduction. "Just feel."

I don't argue when he lifts me and carries me to the desk. As much as I made a deal, I need this. *He* made me need this.

Posing me on the edge, he spreads my legs and steps between them. He reaches over, lifts the lid of an antique silver box, takes out a condom, and hands it to me. As I tear the packet open with my teeth like I saw him do, he rubs a thumb over my clit. My body tightens where he touches me, pleasure already starting to build. My hands shake when I roll the condom over his thick length.

Grabbing a fistful of my hair, he kisses me softly. "How do you want it?"

I don't have to think about it. The tender kiss is sweet, but it makes me inexplicably sad. It's the pull on my hair that makes me wet. "Hard."

He brushes his knuckles over the lace that covers my nipple. "You surprise me, Zoe." He drags his lips over my neck, planting another sweet kiss on my shoulder. "Rough it'll be."

His hands lock around my waist, yanking me flush against him. Impatiently, he moves aside the elastic of my panties and aligns his cock with my entrance. He doesn't move slowly this time. He drives in deep, taking me with a single, hard thrust. I'm wet, but it hurts. It burns. I gasp, embracing the pain, wanting the punishment. He doesn't disappoint. He fucks me like I wanted, so roughly my eyes water and my insides feel raw. He must know I can't handle this pace for long, because he rolls my clit between his fingers until that pain also turns to pleasure, and I come with a wail as relief floods my body. He slams into me while the aftershocks ebb out, and then he climaxes with a grunt.

We're both spent, perspiration beading on our skins. I'm tender when he pulls out, and he's gentle when he picks me up and carries me to the shower. He's careful when he washes me, especially with the part that aches between my legs. He dresses in a tracksuit and I in one of his T-shirts and his robe, and then we have dinner in the formal dining room like two normal people, like the sex in the study never happened.

THE FOLLOWING DAY, Maxime comes home with a tablet on which almost a hundred books are uploaded in English. They range from romance and thrillers to books about clothing design and traveling. I delete the ones about Venice.

Reading brings a measure of relief, but I'm developing cabin fever. I'm lonely, too, being cooped up in the big old house with no one but Francine who goes out of her way to avoid me. The only person I see and speak to is Maxime. I'm losing my concept of time. I don't know what day it is, let alone what hour. I look at my face in the library's antique mirror with a network of cracked spider webs under the glass. I have the odd sensation I'm not real, that life is an illusion slipping through my fingers. The thought scares me. The last thing I can afford is to lose my sanity.

I'm quiet when Maxime comes home, reflecting on this new state of mind. We fuck where he finds me in the library, have a shower, and eat dinner. Now that my body has grown accustomed to being used, he fucks me more often. When we go to bed, he takes me more gently.

Draping me over his chest afterward, he drags a hand through my hair. "What did you do today?"

"Read."

"What did you read?"

"Dunno. Can't remember."

He sweeps my hair over my shoulder, caressing the curve of my neck. "You were reading *Gone with the Wind*. You said it's a long one. Did you finish it?"

"Oh." I rub my cheek over his chest, craving the warmth and contact. "Yes."

"Did you like it?"

I frown. "Mm." The truth is, I can't remember. The words registered but the meaning didn't. I'm filling my brain with empty phrases, with letters and lines that don't form pictures. I'll pay better attention tomorrow. Right after I've written Damian's letter. I write to him every week, saying how happy I am but planting clues about the truth via our code language.

"Zoe?"

"Mm?"

His hand stills on my shoulder. "Did you hear what I said?"

"Sorry, what was that?"

He grips my chin and turns my face toward him. "I said you need exercise."

"Oh. Right." The thought of it alone makes me tired.

"I'll have an indoor bike and walker installed."

"Don't waste your money. I'm not the walker-biker type."

He frowns. "You're pale."

"I have a pale skin."

"Paler than usual. Do you feel sick?"

"I'm fine."

He lets my face go to sweep a hand over my back. "I've tired you out. Go to sleep."

I close my eyes and do exactly that, because I've learned something new.

Avoidance doesn't only come with daydreaming.

The best way to avoid reality is the dreamless state of sleep.

CHAPTER 20

Maxime

She's bored, my little flower. Isolating her in a house far removed from a city and the bustle of life isn't ideal, but the Italian negotiations Alexis so graciously started in my absence is complicated. I'm needed at work now more than ever. I don't trust my brother, and my father is like a fucking child that needs overseeing all the time. Between keeping Alexis in check and making sure my father doesn't sate his greed by doing something stupid like over-charging our Italian connection, I've got my hands full.

I've neglected Zoe. I've neglected her needs. She's shown me she'll be good. She's given me trust. I have to reciprocate by giving her leash a little farther reach. I don't like the idea of my men looking at her, but I've agreed to let her outside. She needs the air and the exercise. She's too pale, too listless. I'm not an idiot. I know what the signs of depression are. I know she's lonely. She needs human contact. I wasn't planning on taking her back to my parents' house, but the lunch on Sunday may be just what she needs.

It's lunchtime when I push the doors of the club open. The usual mob is already there—uncle Emile, my father, and a few of his men, the muscles and specialists. Me, I'm the brain. Benoit and Gautier flank me.

"You're late," my father says, clipping a cigar.

"Traffic." I adjust my jacket and sit. A topless waitress puts an espresso next to me. I push it away. "Where's the contract?"

My father shifts it over the table to me. I flip the pages, scanning over the print to make sure nothing new has been slipped in. I wouldn't put that past my father. I'm at the second-last page when Paolo Zanetti arrives with an entourage of guards. The Italian is short and stocky with shrewd eyes. Thank God the man's daughters take after their mother.

I stand. "Mr. Zanetti."

He shakes my father's hand, then mine.

Taking the pen, I turn to the last page of the contract, but Zanetti grabs my arm before I can sign. He nods at one of his men who puts a ledger on top of the contract.

I eye the gleeful man, addressing him in Italian. "What's this?"

"The new contract."

My father pushes to his feet. "We've negotiated terms."

"The terms have changed," Zanetti says. "I want ten percent extra on everything you move through my territory plus free rights to the Riviera."

"What?" My father pushes his palms on the table.

"We'll take it," I say.

That's a better deal than what I was hoping for. I've been bidding low, knowing Zanetti would come with a counteroffer. I've done my homework. There's nothing Zanetti loves better than winning, not even money, and I've just made him feel like we're the biggest fucking losers on the planet. I've got him by the balls, and he doesn't even know it.

My father clenches his fingers on the edge of the table. He can't challenge me in front of everyone. We have to appear united. Raphael

Belshaw's sincere anger only makes Zanetti smugger, playing right into my hand.

Opening the ledger, I read through the contract, and then sign on the dotted line.

"Wonderful," Zanetti says, snatching up his copy. "I can't wait to take the tour."

"After lunch." I indicate the seat next to me. "I'll show you around. How long are you staying in town?"

"We're leaving tomorrow."

Good. We have a family lunch tomorrow. Inviting Zanetti would've been obligatory.

It's not the kind of trouble I need right now.

CHAPTER 21

Zoe

The house where Maxime parks is not as big as his parents' place, but it's just as imposing. A table with champagne is set out in the foyer. Maxime hangs my coat in the closet next to an array of expensive labels before handing me a glass. I drink it all. I'm nervous about being here, especially after how the last visit with his family went.

He places a palm on my back and lowers his head to whisper in my ear, "We're going to get separated. Men in the lounge, women in the kitchen. Yell if you need me."

I stare up at his face. There's a spark of humor in his gray eyes, an easiness that's unusual for him.

"You look happy with yourself."

"I signed off on a deal. It was a trying negotiation."

"In gemstones?"

He smiles. "No."

"What then?"

He takes my empty glass and puts it back on the table. "Come."

Putting an arm around my waist, he leads me through the foyer to the lounge, which is packed with people. I recognize Cecile and Hadrienne, but none of the others.

His arm tightens around me as we stop in front of a thickset man with a drooping eye. "Zoe, this is my father, Raphael."

Raphael holds out a hand. His expression is neutral, but I get the feeling he doesn't like me.

"My father doesn't speak much English," Maxime says.

"Isn't Belshaw an English surname?" I ask.

"Very French, in fact. One of the oldest."

"Max!" Two women storm up to us, throwing their arms simultaneously around Maxime.

Sandwiched in the middle, he chuckles. "And these are my cousins, Noelle and Sylvie."

The young women turn to me. They both have dark hair and green eyes. They look so much alike, they could've been twins. The only difference between them is that Sylvie is a little taller. They're both wearing Dior, matching vintage dresses with a cinched waist. Noelle's gaze moves over my off-shoulder jersey and jeans. I'm underdressed. This isn't the laid-back Sunday barbecues I'm used to being invited to back home.

Sylvie takes Maxime's arm. "I have to talk to you about something."

She drags him away, leaving me stranded with Noelle. The silence is uncomfortable.

"I'm going to help in the kitchen," Noelle says after a strained moment, slipping past me.

I look over to the terrace where Maxime and Sylvie are talking outside. It looks serious.

Hadrienne approaches me with a stiff back and places her hand on the shoulder of the man who's chatting to Raphael to catch his attention. "This is my husband, Emile."

Emile turns sideways to look at me. He nods but doesn't shake my hand.

"Well," Cecile says, joining our circle. "Look who's here." Pushing past me, she says, "I smell something burning in the kitchen."

"Oh, dear," Hadrienne exclaims, following on her heels.

Emile turns back to his conversation with Raphael. I stand awkwardly, feeling out of place. After another few moments, I don't have a choice but to offer my help in the kitchen.

I go back through the foyer and follow the smell of rosemary and garlic to the kitchen where the women are gathered, talking in French.

I stop in the door. "Can I help with anything?"

They fall quiet. Cecile and Hadrienne exchange a look. Noelle glares at me.

"I suppose you could prepare the coffee tray," Hadrienne says, waving a hand at a coffee maker on the shelf.

The atmosphere is toxic. What have I done? They don't know Maxime is keeping me against my will. As far as they know, we met in South Africa, and now we're together. Why would they hold that against me?

Unable to take the tension any longer, I ask, "Why are you acting like this?"

Cecile tilts her head. "What makes you think we're acting in any way? You're not that important. In fact, you're nothing, neither family nor friend."

My lips part in shock at her blatant hostility. Before I can say anything, the three women carry on with their conversation in French, acting as if I don't exist. I'm tempted to run away, but I won't give them the satisfaction. Instead, I go through the cupboards like I own them until I find the ground coffee and filters. A nasty part of me notices Hadrienne's displeasure with ugly satisfaction. It only spurs me on. I open and close the cupboards loud enough to disturb their talking. Since I don't see any mugs, I take the small espresso cups and place them on a tray with teaspoons and the pot of sugar. I arrange everything just so. There. Only then do I walk from the room.

My chest is tight with tension when I reenter the lounge. The men are nowhere to be seen. Walking out onto the terrace, I lean against the wall and stare into the distance to where the water glitters with sparklers of sun. It's a clear day, sunny and cold. I shiver without my coat.

Sylvie steps out with two glasses of red wine. She holds one out to me. "It's pretty, isn't it?"

I take the drink hesitantly.

"It must be tough," she says.

"What?"

She takes a sip of her wine. "Being the new girl."

"I suppose adaption is always tough," I say vaguely.

"They're cliquish, my family." She smiles. "It's not easy to get in."

"I've noticed."

"You can call me if you'd like to talk or grab a coffee in town."

I look at her in surprise. "Thanks."

"I'm only here until the end of the month before the new semester starts, but feel free to call me in Paris."

"What are you studying?"

"Law. My father isn't happy about it." She laughs. "He thinks I'm wasting my time."

"Why?"

She sits down on the bench. "Because he'll marry me off to some wealthy guy who probably won't allow me to work."

"How can a husband make decisions for his wife?"

She crosses her legs. "This is *le milieu*, baby. It's just how it works." Her gaze trails over me. "I'm not sure what I envy you more for, your ignorance or your freedom."

I look away. How ironic. As for ignorance, there's nothing to envy. She unknowingly takes the prize. She has no idea how wrong she is about my freedom.

"Hey." She gets up and nudges my shoulder. "The men are smoking cigars in the study. They'll be in there for a while. I can bum a cigarette from one of the guards. Want one?"

I think about the night Maxime had taken my virginity. "No, thank you."

"Suit yourself." She pushes off the wall. "Will you cover for me?"

"What should I say?"

"That I'm in the bathroom touching up my makeup or something."

"Sure."

She winks. "I love your outfit, by the way."

"Thanks, I guess."

Backtracking to the steps, she rambles off a number. "That's my telephone number. Remember it. You're going to need a friend to go shopping." She salutes before cutting across the lawn to where a man stands guard.

I'm not ready to go back inside, but I'm cold. I leave the wine on the coffee table. Rubbing my arms, I go over to the mantelpiece and inspect the photos. Most of them are of a younger Sylvie and Noelle.

"Lunch is ready," Noelle calls from somewhere in the house.

Maxime comes to find me, smelling of cigars and winter. He drags his nose through my hair. "What have you been doing with yourself?"

"I spoke to Sylvie." I scan his face for his reaction.

"Good."

"You're not upset?"

He cups my neck and brushes his thumb over my nape. "Why would I be?"

"I didn't think you'd want me to speak to your family."

"Sylvie is a good girl." He kisses my lips. "What I said about Alexis stands."

"Where is he, by the way?"

His face darkens. "Miss him?"

"That's not what I said. I was just wondering."

"No need to waste your wonderings on my brother, little flower."

Taking my hand, he leads me to the dining room. A table is set with the finest porcelain and crystal I've seen. I'm out of my depth, even more so when Hadrienne announces I'll sit between Sylvie and Noelle, separated from Maxime.

I hold onto his hand when he moves to take his seat.

He looks at me. "What is it?"

"What are we eating?" I whisper.

He frowns. "Why?"

I look from under my lashes at the array of knives and forks next to each plate. "I'm not educated in all those eating utensils."

A laugh bursts from his chest. It's loud and uninhibited, and it makes everyone look at us, but he doesn't seem to care.

Lowering his head to my ear, he says in a low voice, "Just follow my lead."

Embarrassed about the room's attention on us, I pull away to take my seat, but he holds me back.

"For the record, Zoe, you're a little uncultured, but you're not uneducated."

Raphael clears his throat. My cheeks are hot when I take my seat. Cecile sits as straight as a statue, her eyes on her plate.

I don't know how I get through the three hour-long, five course ordeal. The only people who speak to me are Maxime and Sylvie. The rest pretend I don't exist. Still, they speak English, which leaves the two older men mostly quiet. The afternoon is a disaster. It was a mistake to bring me.

When the table is cleared, we move to the lounge for coffee. Noelle carries in the tray I've prepared.

"Oh, dear," Cecile says, eyeing the tray.

Noelle giggles.

I look between them. "Is something wrong?"

Sylvie snatches up the sugar pot. "Nothing." She disappears down the hallway and returns with a silver pot filled with sugar cubes.

"That's such an Anglo Saxon thing," Cecile says.

Hadrienne lights a cigarette. "Don't get me started on the clothes."

Maxime stands. "Emile, Hadrienne, thank you for lunch."

"You're leaving?" Hadrienne asks. "Already?"

Maxime takes my hand and helps me to my feet. "We have a long way home."

It takes almost thirty minutes to say goodbye, and by the time we get in the car I'm emotionally exhausted. I don't want to repeat one of these lunches any time soon.

"Did you enjoy yourself?" Maxime asks as he turns the car onto the coastal road.

"It was nice meeting Sylvie."

"I've been busy with work, but now that the deal's done, we'll go out more." He takes my hand. "I promise."

I give him a sideway glance. "You don't have to make an effort. It's not like we're dating."

"I said I'd look out for you if you behave, and you've been behaving very well."

I scoff. "I'm glad you approve."

"Don't spoil it now."

"I've been thinking."

He smiles. "What has been going through my little flower's mind?"

"I want to learn to speak French."

He raises a brow. "I didn't expect that."

"Will you teach me?"

He lifts my hand to his lips and kisses my knuckles. "I can do better. I'll get you a tutor."

"Really?"

"Of course."

"Why would you do that for me?"

"Because I can. Why do you want to speak French?"

I shrug. "Because I can." So that no one can talk about me behind my back ever again.

His eyes darken but the humor remains in his voice. "You and that sassy mouth of yours. I can think of ways to tame it, and I'm not going to hold out until we're home."

Clenching the wheel with one hand, he pulls down his zipper with the other and frees his cock. Seeing him so hard for me just from a game of words makes me horny and wet. When he cups the back of my neck, I go down on him willingly, swallowing him like he taught me. I swirl my tongue around the head and suck until my cheeks hollow. He curses, saying filthy words in French. I don't need a tutor to understand those. I take the power he gives. I own the groan that erupts from his chest. I own his release.

CHAPTER 22

Maxime

I watch Zoe through the open door of the dressing room while buttoning up my shirt. She sits in front of the dresser, applying her makeup. Her hair is twisted on her head in pretty curls. She's wearing a red dress with black heels, and the diamonds I gave her in Venice as a gift to commemorate our first time shines in her ears. She's a vision. It's hard tearing my gaze away to fit my cufflinks.

I check my watch. We have an hour before the dinner. It's a charity event to raise money for cancer research. I hate these galas, but I'm hoping it'll do Zoe good. She objected, said she didn't want to go, but she needs to be around people.

Now that the Italian deal has been negotiated, I can focus on her again. I feel both lighter and heavier. We need the alliance with the Italians. It gives us access to their infrastructure, a broadened scope to move our diamonds safely, while the tax they're paying to ship from our port doesn't hurt, either. We've been at war for too long, wiping out each other's men and resources. Hence, the deal is a good thing. Complicated, but good. It's going to require some finesse in the foreseeable future. In the short term, it means I can spend more time with my flower.

Yesterday's lunch didn't go as well as I've hoped. The men owe Zoe the respect she deserves as my lover. It's an unbendable rule. However, I didn't foresee how the women would react. I can't really blame them. Of course, they'd frown upon her sharing my bed. Mistresses are a common occurrence among the menfolk in our circles, but you don't bring them to a family lunch. A charity event, yes. A weekend in the Bahamas, definitely. While mistresses wear diamonds and sip champagne on yachts, the wives are home raising their cheating husband's kids. I'd hoped Maman would've been more open-minded, if not for Zoe then for my sake, but I'd misjudged my mother's tolerance and Catholic values. For as staunch as her values are, her tolerance is low.

I still don't know why Alexis didn't show. If I haven't fucked Zoe from the minute we got home to sunrise, I would've called him. He's probably scheming behind my back like he tried to weasel his way into the Italian deal. Taking my phone from my pocket, I send a text to Gautier, telling him to tail my brother and find out what he's so busy with that's more important than a family lunch. For all the times the married men in my family have entertained their lovers on exotic islands and faraway dream escapes, they don't back out when there's a family lunch at home. Another one of our unspoken rules.

"I'm ready," Zoe says.

I lift my head to look at her. The breath is knocked from my lungs. The dress clings to her body, accentuating her curves. The gown was my choice. I know she hates it, but she has no idea what a knockout she is with her slender neck and the milky skin of her shoulders exposed. There's a flush on her cheeks again since she started taking long walks outside. Her skin and eyes glow, the freckles on her nose like a dusting of golden stars. She's the epitome of innocence and purity. Only, I know she likes sex both sweet and rough. I know how to read her, how to give her what she needs, and I burn with satisfaction knowing I'm the one who corrupted her. Her moans and dirty little acts are all mine.

"I don't know about this," she says, smoothing her palms over her hips. "I really don't like these formal parties."

I take her wrap from the chair and drape it around her shoulders. "So you've said."

"I should stay. I'd rather watch a movie here where it's warm."

"Not an option." Hooking my arm through hers, I lead her downstairs. "I want to show you off." Every man in Marseille and to the ends of the world needs to understand she's mine. No one will ever stake a claim on her again, no man in the mob, and no man outside of the families. No one will be foolish enough.

Her spine stiffens. "I'm not a showpiece."

"You are whatever I want you to be."

She pulls to a stop. "I don't want to be auctioned."

"It's for charity."

"What happens after the bidding?"

"You dance with the highest bidder."

"Just a dance?"

Unfortunately, no. Mostly not. The high society of Marseille enjoys a bit of swinging while raising money for a good cause.

She yanks on my sleeve. "Is the winner going to expect sex?"

"Most probably."

Her nostrils flare. "Is this why you dressed me up like a slut?"

"Careful, Zoe. One, you look beautiful, and two, you should really remember to trust me."

"To trust you to whore me out?"

A nerve pinches between my shoulder blades. We were doing so well with her obeying me blindly. I grip her arm. "You're not a whore, and I'm not tempted to make one of you."

Her words are spoken breathlessly. "You already have."

My anger starts to simmer. A curl slips loose from her updo as I shake her. "Take that back."

"I can't." Tears pool in her eyes, giving them that expressive edge I love so much. "I can't take back my virginity."

Bringing that up now makes me angrier, because I don't like how she puts it. I don't like how she sees it.

"We made a deal," I say through clenched teeth.

"Exactly." She stares up at me, fearless but wary. "For which I'm paying with my body. Tell me that doesn't make me your whore."

I shake her harder. More curls fall to her shoulders. "It's nothing like that."

"If that's what you believe, you're lying to yourself."

I march her backward with a palm on her chest and slam her body against the wall. "When have I ever treated you like a whore?"

"Whores get paid." Emotions swirl in her eyes, teardrops trapped behind a brilliant blue. "You're paying me with my brother's life."

Grabbing her neck, I fold my fingers around the slender column. "You'll be wise to shut up now, Zoe."

Her chest heaves with breaths. Her palms are pressed flat on the wall next to her hips. She's scared, but she doesn't back off. She keeps on fucking pushing me. "Can't face the truth? The diamonds, the clothes, the tutor, what are they if not payment?"

I squeeze harder. "Gifts. Fucking gifts, you unthankful little—"

She lifts her chin, defying the hold than can snap her neck. "Say it."

Goddamn. My grip slackens.

"Go ahead," she says. "Finish what you were going to say."

"Bitch," I grit out, my whole body shaking with anger. "You unthankful little bitch."

Fuck dammit. It's true. Every word she said is chiseled down to its naked, hurtful truth. I made her a whore, but a cherished one. Alexis would've done so much worse.

Her body sags against the wall, her tiny frame crumbling. "Is this what showing me off means?" She sweeps a hand over the dress. "I look pretty for your friends? You share me when the mood hits?"

Slamming a palm next to her face on the wall, I lean in. "You don't know me, remember? *If* I'm ever inclined to share, you'll do as I tell you, and you'll do it with a smile on your face. If I tell you to swallow my best friend's cock and take it in your pussy and up your ass, you'll do that, too."

I don't have a best friend, and I'd rather saw off my dick than share her, but she doesn't need to know that. She doesn't deserve the power of that kind of knowledge. What she does need to know by now is to fucking trust me. I guess we have a few more lessons to go.

Her blue eyes are awash with anger. "You're an asshole."

No arguing that fact. It's the hurt in those pretty baby blues that hits me squarely in the chest.

"We're going to be late." I grip her wrist and drag her behind me, my earlier good mood down the drain.

She doesn't say a word as we get into the car and drive to Marseille. She stares from her window at the dark landscape. I clench the wheel so hard the ring with our family crest, the same one my father wears, presses a groove into my finger. It's the ring the head of the family wears, the man who makes the decisions. The weight of it leaves a mark on my soul. Of all the sins I've committed, Zoe is the biggest one, the stone that drags me under and drowns me. She consented, but I didn't give her a choice. The only choice I gave her was how to look at the situation, how to see herself. I wanted to give her pretty, and she had to go choose the ugly truth.

Fuck.

I slam the wheel. Zoe jumps. She huddles closer to the door, her shoulders turned away from me. I want to remind her of that choice, but it'll be a lie dressed up in glitter, in diamonds and red, and it looks like Zoe is done pretending. She's done living in a dream.

As paparazzi are flocking the main entrance to the casino, we use a back entrance. I promised my father I'd be discreet. The casino belongs to a distant uncle. The annual charity event is held in the big hall. I greet a few people, mostly business associates, and introduce Zoe as my date. She's tense on my arm. I'm still angry, too angry to set her at ease. Where I was looking forward to bringing her here only an hour ago, I now wish this night was already over.

"Max." A sickeningly handsome man with dark hair, brown eyes, and an olive skin tone pats me on the shoulder. "Good to see you," he says in French.

Fuck. Paolo Zanetti's son. We've only met once. It was a couple of years ago when we had our first talks about making a French-Italian connection. He's one of Zanetti's specialists, a genius at money laundering. At twenty-seven, he's young for the high position he holds in their organization, but I respect his brains. I hate his pretty face though, and when he smiles at Zoe, I downright detest it.

What the fuck is he doing here? There can only be one reason.

"I didn't know you accompanied your father," I say, barely holding the ice from my tone.

"I'm getting to know our new partners." His brown eyes tighten the minutest fraction when he turns them to Zoe. "Aren't you going to introduce me to your lovely companion?"

I switch to English. "This is Zoe. Zoe, this is Leonardo, a business associate."

Taking Zoe's hand, he asks, "Zoe who?"

"Zoe Hart," she says, not knowing the man looking at her with such kindness is a snake about to strike.

"Leonardo Zanetti." He brings Zoe's hand to his lips, intelligently not making contact with her skin. "It's an honor, Zoe. However did this brute catch such a beauty?"

"We met in South Africa during a business trip," I say quickly. Directing my gaze to where he's clutching Zoe's fingers in his paw, I make sure he sees the warning in my eyes.

"If you don't mind me asking," he finally drops Zoe's hand to motion between her and me, "is this casual or serious, because if it's not serious I'd love to meet up in town before I head back to Italy. I've always wanted to go to South Africa, and I could use some travel advice." He turns to me, all false respect. "Of course, if it's serious, I'm not going risk your jealousy, Max."

Zoe glances at me. There's no way she can answer that question. If she says it's not serious, she's accepting his offer. If she says it's serious, she's admitting to something neither she nor I can confess. Something I definitely shouldn't admit to Leonardo Zanetti.

He's pushing me into a corner. Clever motherfucker. I wish I could plant my fist between his troubadour eyes. The only thing preventing me is my strong control, something that has started unraveling earlier tonight. If I'm honest about it, it's been unraveling ever since I've abducted Zoe. I shouldn't let my emotions get the better of me. It'll kill our business. There's too much at stake. I'm about to say Zoe isn't available—indefinitely—when she speaks.

"We're kind of, uh, committed."

Leonardo gives me a smug smile. "I suppose you have to enjoy it while you can."

A tall woman with an athletic build makes her way over with two glasses of champagne. She's dressed in a black number with a slit that starts on her hip.

I tilt my head in the direction of the woman who's heading straight for Leonardo. "Like you are?"

"Oh." He straightens his bowtie. "I'm not committed to anyone. She's just my date for tonight."

"Well, hello," the woman says, shoving a glass in Leonardo's hand. Her eyes roam over Zoe. "You're a pretty little thing."

I put an arm around Zoe's waist and pull her against my side. "We'll go find our table and let you mingle."

"We're at the same table." Leonardo raises his glass. "Let me show you."

Of course, we are. With the newly forged deal, Leonardo is as good as family, part of my clan. Clenching my jaw, I follow them to our table.

We greet the other people, my cousin, Jerome, as well as an elderly court official and his young fiancée, but I hardly pay them attention. I'm too busy listening in on the conversation between Zoe and Leonardo. They talk about safaris and wine farms, and then about Tuscany. I only relax when Jerome demands Leonardo's attention and Zoe starts talking to Leonardo's date.

My hand wanders to Zoe's thigh under the table. I need the physical reassurance of her presence as much as I need her to understand who's in charge. She stiffens at the gesture, her hand tightening on her water glass. The court official, a man called Big Ben for his unusual height and weight, is staring openly at her. It takes everything I have and some to not crush his skull with the bottle of champagne.

There are speeches about research developments between the courses of salmon terrine, sea bass, and strawberry mousse. I donated handsomely. Ploughing money back into the community keeps doors open for us. It helps make the influential corporate players and government officials turn their heads the other way where our illegal business is concerned.

Zoe pushes the food around on her plate. During the meal, she downs two glasses of champagne, and when the MC announces the start of the auction, she's like a rice paper kite in a storm, looking as if her wings are about to be ripped off.

The sponsors—lovers or spouses—who volunteered the women participating in the auction proudly present their protégés when the MC calls their names. When it's Zoe's turn, I stand and offer her my hand.

She stares up at me with defiant eyes. There's a moment's hesitation, a moment of mistrust when her hate for me is written so clearly on her face it spears my unfeeling heart. I narrow my eyes in warning. If she defies me in front of all these people, I'll make her pay in so many ways she'll wish she'd never brought that lesson upon herself. My pulse beats in my temples as another second passes and the MC clears his throat. Just when I think Zoe is going to decline, she slips her small hand into mine.

I pull her to her feet, my face decorated with the smile I've adopted for the gentry, but the gesture goes no further than my mouth. Behind my tightly stretched lips, my teeth are clenched. Zoe's hesitation only lasted a moment, but a moment is long enough, especially for the sharp eyes of the predators surrounding us. I thought I'd made better progress with my flower, but it seems I've underestimated her. She may need a stronger hand.

Lifting her arm, I turn her in a circle. The hall breaks out in applause. Men nod enthusiastically while women stare daggers. In the midst of salivating wolves and hateful envy stands an innocent little lamb, my virgin sacrifice.

"Fifty," someone calls from the back before the MC has even opened the bidding.

It's what I wanted, for everyone to see who owns her, but the over-eager interest makes my hackles rise. Laughter erupts. Someone pats the impatient bidder on the back. Red-hot jealousy burns in my gut.

"Since the bidding seems to be open," the MC says with a chuckle, "who'd like—"

"One hundred," someone calls.

I turn around. The actor is a national celebrity.

Zoe looks at me quickly. One hundred thousand is the highest bid of the evening yet.

"One hundred and fifty," a fat parliament member says.

Zoe's eyes are burning on my face. I'm not looking at her, but I can feel her stare, her plea.

"Going once," the MC calls.

She lays a hand on my arm, her fingers digging into my skin.

Don't worry, my little flower. Be quiet and learn your lesson in trust.

"Going twice." The MC lifts his hammer.

"Two hundred," I say.

Zoe's chest deflates. Her relief is so great her body sags against mine.

A strong voice with an accent reverberates through the space. "Five hundred."

The room goes quiet. All heads turn toward the owner of the voice. I isolate him in my vision like a torpedo homes in on a target. Our eyes meet across the table.

Leonardo.

There's a challenge in his, a deviant intention. I want to squash him like a bug. My body tenses, every muscle preparing to rip him apart when Jerome's hand falls on my shoulder.

"Don't let him get to you," Jerome whispers.

No. I'm not going to let him get to me. Neither is he getting Zoe. Over my dead body.

"She's not worth it," Jerome continues. "Not the Italian deal."

Wrong fucking words. I shake him off. "One million."

Gasps sound around the room. Zoe stares at me with big eyes, her lush lips parted.

"Wow, uh..." The MC gives a high-pitched laugh. "That sets a new record. I have one million euros for Miss Zoe Hart. Do I have one million and one?"

Leonardo shakes his head at the MC, but his smile is aimed at me. Instead of looking slain, he appears victorious.

"One million going to Mr. Belshaw."

Jerome looks at me as if I've lost my marbles. If only he knew. I would've paid two million. I would've given everything I own to keep another man's hands off the woman I've claimed. Mission accomplished. The message was dealt. Zoe belongs to me. She doesn't know it, but I've just painted a big hands-off sign all over her delectable body. She'll be mine for all eternity.

The lights dim and music comes on. A disco ball throws shards of light over the floor. The MC declares the dance floor open. People stare at us as sponsors lead their protégés to the men who won their bids.

"I believe this dance is mine," I say, pulling Zoe with me to the floor.

She blinks. "Why did you do this?"

"You preferred Leonardo?" My tone is mocking, but there's nothing mocking about the notion driving like a splinter under my skin, that a woman like her would want a man like him. I bet he's the kind of handsome that featured in her dreams, those pretty dreams she exchanged for the cold, hard truth. Me.

Before she can answer, Leonardo walks into my personal space. "Thank you." He leans closer. "You showed me what I wanted to know." Bumping my shoulder, he walks off into the milling crowd.

My skull pricks when I draw Zoe close.

"What's that about?" Zoe asks, her eyes as round as earlier when I had her pushed up against the wall.

"Nothing."

I put my arm around her waist and lead her to the center of the floor where several couples are already dancing. It's a slow dance. I'm a good dancer, courtesy of my mother who insisted on sending me to dance classes when I dropped out of piano lessons. A refined education has always been important to Maman.

Zoe misses the first step. She trips, bracing herself with her palms on my chest. I catch her around the waist to straighten her and lower my head to whisper in her ear, "Relax. Just follow."

Uncertainly, she places her palm in mine and lays a hand on my shoulder. I lead us into the two-step, enjoying the closeness of her body and the familiar smell of roses in her hair. A few tendrils still fall around her face from our earlier fight. She's always pretty, but she's stunning when she's disheveled.

She pulls back to look at me. "Why did you do that?"

"You know why."

"You could've just told me you were going to bid on me. You made me stress all night. Why be so cruel?"

"You know why, Zoe."

"To teach me to trust you?"

Cupping her head, I press her cheek to my chest. "Always."

Our bodies sway to the rhythm, the curves of her small one fitting to the hollows of mine. She fills the emptiness and brings light to my darkness, but when she doesn't trust me, she creates that gaping emptiness that brings out the monster in me.

I'm hard for her. Too hard. I'm not myself, not one hundred percent in control. It's a combination of factors. It's my jealousy. It's our fight. What Leonardo said is pulsing in my brain. Zoe's hesitation needs to be punished. I can't let her relapse go unanswered. Actions have consequences. She said so herself. What respect will she have for me if I'm not a man of my word? Most of all, it's how she sees herself, as nothing but my whore.

When the dance is over, I take her arm and lead her across the hall. The other couples are dispersing, some moving in the same direction as us—to the bedrooms upstairs.

Before we reach the door, Jerome stops me. "You've made a mistake, cousin," he says in French.

I raise a brow. "Have I?"

Zoe looks between us with a frown marring her beautiful features.

"You've just showed everyone the woman means something to you."

Something may be a bit of an understatement. "Good night, Jerome. I'll catch up with you tomorrow."

He shakes his head as we walk off, clearly not impressed with me.

"Where are we going?" Zoe asks when I usher her into the elevator.

We could've just gone home, but I don't want her to have negative connotations to the place I want her to consider as her safe haven.

She follows me out on the top floor, blindly this time. Too little, too late. Blind obedience won't serve her now.

At the presidential suite, I swipe the access card and step aside to let her in. She looks around much like she had that first night in South Africa. The view over the city is stunning.

Turning to me, she asks with a shaky voice, "Why are we here?"

I turn the lock. "Strip."

"You're going to fuck me?"

"I paid a million euros for your pussy. I'm going to make sure I get my money's worth."

Hurt contorts her features. "Why are you doing this, Maxime?"

Advancing on her, I grab a fistful of her hair and pull her head back. "To show you what it's like to be treated like a whore."

"Please." She grips my forearms, her neck straining from my hold on her hair. "Don't do this."

"I'm done talking."

She stumbles as I let her go. Before she falls on her ass, I catch her arm and fling her around. She cries out as I walk her to the window and plaster her body against it. She fights me, but I easily grab her wrists in one hand behind her back and pin her to the pane with my hips while I use my free hand to pull the zipper of her dress down. I shove it over her hips to pool around her feet. With the low back of the dress, she couldn't wear a bra. Her bare breasts press flat against the glass. I rip away the flimsy thong and let it fall on top of the dress. Then I work a knee between her legs, spreading them apart.

"Maxime, please."

I don't listen to the tremor in her voice. I unzip my pants, not bothering to push it over my hips. My cock is ready. Her body isn't, but that's the point of this lesson. That's how whores are treated, without consideration for their pain or pleasure. Taking the base of my cock in my hand, I press the head against her tight opening and thrust inside. She cries out, her face scrunching up and her eyes pinching closed.

She's warm and almost unbearably tight. A hiss leaves her lips as I pull back, bend my knees, and slam my hips up again, claiming my million-euro pussy, showing her the difference between being my lover and my whore. She thought she'd seen that side of me? Not even close.

I fuck her hard, knowing she's dry. My lust mounts, feeding the dark cravings I usually keep in check for her. My breathing is heavy when I unfasten my buckle and pull my belt through the loops. Excitement courses through my veins when I fold the leather double in one hand and pin her wrists hard against her lower back.

"Maxime." Her voice is panicked. "What are you doing?"

"Quiet."

I pull out of her body and take a step away. The head of my cock is slick with pre-cum. I've already gone too far. With any other woman, I would've put a condom on before I started. Zoe is my exception. She's the only woman I've ever fucked bareback. Taking a rubber from my pocket, I sheathe my cock and drop the packet on the carpet, not caring where it falls.

She knows what's going to happen. Still, she deserves a fair warning. I drag the belt over her ass, following the line of the enticing curve. She's toned and round, an ass made for spanking and fucking.

Taking aim, I swing my arm back. The leather makes a hissing sound as it cuts through the air. It falls with a sharp crack on her skin. She sucks air in loudly, her globes clenching and her body flattening against the glass to escape the pain. I don't spare her. I pull back and lash her again, carefully controlling my strength. Red welts mar her porcelain skin. I don't like to see them there. I don't like spoiling what's perfect, but she left me no choice. I have to prove that I'm trustworthy, that I make good on my promises. I can be as cruel as I can be kind. She must learn this lesson about choice.

She's fighting me, twisting and bucking, but it doesn't take much to keep her pinned to the window.

"Keep still," I say against her ear, "and this will be over quicker."

"Please." Her breath catches on a hitch. "Please, stop."

"I'm afraid not yet, *ma belle*."

With the next lash, I hit her like I mean it. It makes me harder. It's the depraved part of me that enjoys inflicting pain when I torture my enemies. It's the twisted excitement I feel at killing.

Tears roll over her cheeks, but she's brave. She doesn't give in. She remains on her feet. I dip my fingers between her legs. She's still dry. It doesn't stop me from entering her with three fingers. Stretching her with my hand is the only mercy I give her before I shove my cock back into her tight little cunt, greedily taking everything I've paid for. If she's my whore, this is how it is. This is about me. I don't owe her anything other than the price we agreed on. I honored my end of the bargain. She'll honor hers.

My lust is burning white-hot. The violence brings that out in me. I fuck her so hard the breath leaves her lungs in a feminine whimper with every thrust. It's a grueling pace, and it's not enough. Yet she's growing slicker.

Brushing away the tendrils of hair that stick to the sweaty skin of her neck, I nip the soft flesh where her shoulder starts. "Such a naughty little slut. You're getting wet. You like it when I'm rough."

Her nails dig into my skin of my hands where I'm restraining her. "Don't do this."

I gather her arousal and spread it to her asshole. "You're a dirty little whore, and I'm going to fuck every hole I paid for."

She gasps. "Maxime, please."

I slap her ass hard. "Don't you dare say my name. Whores call me Mr. Belshaw."

Pulling her globes apart, I admire the rosebud pucker of her ass, the forbidden entrance I have every right to take. Using her arousal as a lubricant is more than what I would've given any other whore. Still, she's a virgin, so I spit in my palm and coat her well before sinking a finger through the tight ring of muscle. Her inner muscles grip me like fist. When I start pumping, she whimpers. It's when I add a second finger that she fights. She only wiggles and twists until I remove my fingers and press my cock on her dark entrance. Then she stills. I use the moment to press forward, applying pressure until her muscles relent and her ass swallows the head of my cock.

It's a beautiful sight. Her globes are glowing red and her asshole stretching to take my cock. Her pussy is dripping wet. Arousal glistens on her clit. The bud is dark pink and engorged. I could easily slam all the way up, hurt her and get off on her screams. But this is her first time, and I don't want her to keep bad connotations.

Instead, I pull out of her ass, spin her around, and push her down to her knees. I bury one hand in her hair while I use the other to get rid of the rubber. Then I spear through her lips and down her throat. I don't deep-throat her like the first time. I just use her mouth to come. I do it fast, relief surging through me as I shoot my load on her tongue and mess up her face with my cum, but I don't find calm. The anger and darkness linger.

She's served her purpose. I let her go. She's sucking in deep breaths, trembling on her knees. Her mascara and lipstick are smeared; her cheeks and lips streaked with my cum.

"Stay," I say.

I go to the bathroom, wash up, and adjust my clothes. When I come back, she's still on her knees on the carpet with her back against the exposed window.

I stop in front of her. "That's a good slut. Do you want to come?"

She looks broken, her eyelashes wet with tears.

I crouch down in front of her. "You do, don't you? That's what dirty whores want. Go ahead. Touch yourself."

Her lips part as she stares at me with a mixture of shock and hurt.

I chuckle. "You didn't think I was going to touch you like that, did you?"

Her chin trembles but her voice is strong. "You're a bastard."

I shrug. "It's your choice. Get up."

Using the window as a support, she pushes herself up.

"What did this lesson teach you, Zoe?"

She hugs her breasts and crosses her legs, hiding as much of her nakedness as she can. "That nothing we've shared is real," she bites out with tears shining in her eyes. "The kindness isn't real. It means nothing, which means this means nothing, too." Spitting the words at me, she continues, "You mean nothing to me, and you never will."

It's my turn to stare at her. I don't like it. I don't like it one bit that she thinks what I've given her isn't real. It's true, though. Isn't that what I said to my father, that I was going to manipulate her into wanting to stay by giving her what she wants?

I've underestimated her, but not as much as I've underestimated how her answer would affect me. This isn't how this lesson was supposed to go at all.

Gnashing my teeth, I say, "Make your choice, Zoe. My lover or my whore?"

She's trembling, her frail body shaking, but from the way she drops her arms and stands up straighter as she bravely exposes herself, I know what her answer is going to be. She's going to choose the spiteful route.

My phone rings just as she opens her mouth to speak. I take it out of my pocket and check the screen. It's Gautier.

I answer with, "Not now."

"It's your brother, sir," he says. "You better come now."

CHAPTER 23

Zoe

"Put on your dress," Maxime says in a curt tone.

The string of expletives he utters makes me rethink disobeying him in this. Something happened. He doesn't wait to see if I'm complying. He hurries to the door and yanks it open. Standing there waiting, he drags a hand over his head. I've never seen Maxime behaving so worried. Angry, yes. Cold and cruel, yes, but never with such obvious concern.

I shimmy into the dress as quickly as I can. Anyone can walk past the open door, but I also instinctively know whatever the phone call was about is bigger than this, than me. The fabric is light, but even the soft brush against my backside hurts. The ache between my legs and in my dark entrance is an extension of my punishment as I walk over to where my captor waits.

He looks at me as if seeing me for the first time. "You're a mess. Grab a towel from the bathroom."

I do as he says. My reflection in the mirror shocks me to a standstill. My makeup is smudged, and my hair is wild. Streaks of cum are mixed with dark rivulets of mascara on my cheeks. Shame burns in the pit of my stomach. Tears burn behind my eyes. Who am I becoming?

Maxime's loud voice booms through the space, making me jump. "Now, Zoe."

Grabbing a facecloth, I wet it with cold water and rub it over my face until my skin turns red. Not everything comes off, so I bring it with me to wipe away the evidence of what I can't face. Maxime's expression is tight. He's taken off his jacket. At the door, he holds the jacket out for me. I pull it on, hating the smell of winter that clings to the fabric.

Taking my hand, he pulls me behind him to the elevator. I almost trip in my heels trying to keep up. We ride down straight to the basement parking, not going back for our coats or my clutch in the cloakroom.

He unlocks the car and shoves me inside. "Buckle up."

Sitting hurts my butt. I shift to the most comfortable position I can find. Before I've fastened my seatbelt, Maxime is already pulling out of the parking with screeching tires. His hands are clenched on the wheel and his shoulders tense. When we hit the road, I understand why he told me to buckle up. He's driving like a daredevil, breaking the speed limit. I have to grab onto the door handle to prevent my body from being thrown to his side as we round a bend.

On a straight stretch of road, I rub the cloth over my face again, but I don't dare look in the sun visor mirror. I'm not sure I can cope with what I'll see.

Maxime doesn't say a word. All of his attention is fixed on the road. Fortunately, he's a skilled driver. We skip several red lights. I'm waiting with my stomach pulled tight for a police siren to sound or for us to crash into another car, but nothing happens. I'm one big ball of nerves when he finally parks in front of an apartment block near the harbor.

"Come," he says, throwing open his door.

I get out and scurry after him to the entrance. Gautier stands there, a dark look on his face. They exchange a few words. Gautier nods, then takes off.

Maxime punches in a code and lets me in.

"Where are we?" I ask, looking around the modern lobby.

His voice is tight. "My brother's place."

I want to ask what we're doing here, but a voice in the back of my head tells me this isn't the moment for questions. An unsettling sensation steals over me. Alexis seemed nice enough when I met him, but I'm sure it was all acting, just like Maxime is always acting with me, playing nice or decent and kind when it's nothing but a show, a sick game to manipulate me.

Maxime and I climb into the elevator. He punches in another code and watches the floors light up with a broody expression. Alexis's apartment is on the top floor. The elevator gives direct access to Alexis's lounge. We step into a spacious room with futon sofas and a low table. A lamp casts a soft light over the wooden floor. An electric fire burns in a black metal pit in the center. It's all very cozy, but goosebumps break out over my skin. The hair on my neck pricks. Something isn't right.

Alexis stands in front of the window that overlooks the harbor with his back turned to us and a drink in his hand.

"Alexis." Maxime's deep voice thunders through the space.

Alexis turns around, unsteady on his feet. Is he drunk?

Maxime advances on him with big steps. "What the fuck have you done?"

A whimpering noise comes from somewhere down the hallway. The sound makes me stop breathing. There's something horrifying about it, something that's not right. It's the sound a wounded animal would make. It's hopeless and scared, lost in pain.

Maxime grabs Alexis by the collar of his shirt. "*Qu'est-ce que tu as fait?*"

Alexis stumbles, spilling his drink over Maxime's sleeve. He says something in French that makes Maxime draw back an arm and punch him in the face. Alexis goes down on his ass, the glass flying through the air and breaking in shards on the floor.

The violence is unsettling enough, bringing back unpleasant memories of my drunken father I don't care to play over in my mind. My reaction is involuntary, a flashback to my youth that makes me retreat to the corner and try to make myself invisible, but it's not Maxime's pounding fists that hold my attention. It's the sickening grunts dispersed with pitiful moaning coming from elsewhere. Maxime is straddling his brother, dealing punch after punch to his jaw. My whole body drawn tight, I turn away from the fight and pause in the doorway. A low howl makes my stomach turn. Cold sweat breaks out over my body.

Light spills from a room at the end of the hallway. My mind screams for me to hurry, but my feet refuse to obey. It's as if I'm stuck in slow motion, in a very bad dream. When I finally reach the open door from where the light and sounds come, I battle to take in the scene. My brain refuses to process it. Nausea boils in my stomach, and bile pushes up in my throat.

A naked woman is tied to a cross in the middle of the floor, hands and feet spread. A man is pounding into her. He doesn't see me, because his back is turned to the door. A horrible pattern of crisscrossing lines covers what I can see of her breasts and thighs, blood dripping from the cuts. Her left arm is bent unnaturally at the elbow. Her face is bruised and her eyes swollen shut. Cuts mar her legs and feet.

My God. I swallow and swallow again. I've never seen anything as gruesome. The shock that froze me fizzles into a fit of blinding rage. My gaze settles on a whip that lies on a bed covered with a plastic sheet. I move like a demon, grabbing the instrument of torture from the bed and swinging it with all my might at the naked man's back.

He freezes with a curse at the fall of the strap, his eyes wild and confused as he turns his head my way. He shouts something violent in French as he rips free from the woman and charges for me. The lash I dealt hadn't drawn blood. To do so is harder than I thought. Lifting my arm, I put more effort into it as I swing the whip his direction, bringing it down over his face and chest.

He utters a cry, followed by a curse. Before I have time to hit him again, he's on me, wrestling the whip from my hand.

"Let her go," a frighteningly cold, hard voice says from the door.

The man stills. A sliver of fear slips into his voice. "Monsieur Belshaw?"

When he obliges, I rush to the woman. Maxime's words are murderous. The man starts pleading.

"It's okay," I whisper when I reach the woman. "I'm going to untie you."

She can't see me through her swollen eyes, but at the sound of my voice she starts sobbing.

"You're going to be all right," I say, working on the rope that ties her right wrist.

It's knotted too tightly. My fingers are shaking too much. I look around the room for something I can use when Maxime pushes me out of the way. He's clutching a big carving knife.

"Fuck," he mumbles under his breath as he takes in the woman.

"What are you doing with the knife?" I ask, placing myself between him and the woman.

"Cutting her loose. Move out of the way."

I step aside, casting a glance at the door, but the naked man is gone.

Maxime cuts through the rope tied around her wrist.

"I think her arm is broken." I'm having a hard time keeping my voice even. "I'm calling an ambulance."

"No."

His harsh tone makes me pause. "She needs to go to a hospital."

"She will. Put an arm under her shoulder. She's going to need support when I cut her loose."

I wiggle my arm between the cross and her back, holding her up as best as I can while Maxime frees her arms and legs. My heart is pounding between my ribs, my breathing erratic, but I push everything else to the back and focus on helping this poor woman.

Who does something like this? Alexis is ten times worse of a monster than the man who claimed me.

"Go find me a blanket," Maxime says, lifting the limp woman into his arms. "Second door on the left."

I rush down the hallway and push open the door Maxime has indicated. It's dark. I fumble for a light switch. When I find the button, I flick it on. It's a bedroom. The sheets are tangled on the bed. It smells of whiskey and sex. A blanket lies discarded on the floor. Snatching it up, I run back to the room at the end. Maxime exits just as I arrive. I cover the woman's body as best as I can.

"Let's go," Maxime says tersely.

I follow him down the hallway. Through the doorway of the lounge, I see Alexis and the other man. The stranger is dressed, and Alexis is holding a bag of frozen peas against his eye. I get the door and the elevator while Maxime carries the woman and says soothing things to her in French even if she seems unconscious.

Downstairs in the street, Gautier, who's returned, jumps to attention. He gets the passenger door while Maxime lowers the woman onto the seat and secures her safety belt. He says something to Gautier, then races around the car, gets in, and starts the engine. I watch dumbfounded, my words all dried up, as he takes off like a racing devil, the taillights of his car two red eyes in a dark evil of the night.

"I'm taking you home," Gautier says.

I turn to face him. At first his words don't make sense. Nothing makes sense. I'm shivering in Maxime's jacket, but not from cold.

"Come, Miss Hart. Please."

I look at his outstretched arm. A realization dawns on me. I don't know how I figure it out because the dots from my mind to my thoughts won't connect. He's not allowed to touch me.

"Please," he says again.

Numb, I follow him to a car parked on the side of the road and get in when he holds the door for me. I can't breathe. I can't calm the frantic beat of my heart. For the first time since Maxime took me from my home and brought me here, I'm grateful to my kidnapper. I'm grateful he didn't hand me over to his brother.

What I've seen tonight changes everything. It changes the answer I was going to give Maxime back at the hotel.

CHAPTER 24

Maxime

On the way to the hospital, I call Dr. Olivier.

"Another one?" he asks curtly when I've explained the situation.

"I know." I glance at the unconscious woman. "This is ending tonight."

He sighs. "I'll meet you there in ten."

I park underground and take the elevator to the ground floor. It's late. It's quiet. Dr. Olivier meets me at the side entrance. Together, we install the woman in a private room. The good doctor will treat her and give her something for the pain. He'll also handle the tricky logistics of the paperwork.

I take a picture of her injuries with my phone. Pocketing it, I say, "Text me an update on her progress."

The doctor looks up from examining her. "Where are you going?"

"To deal with my brother."

He nods. It's not his place to ask questions. "Do you know her identity? I'll need a name for the forms."

I'll need it to pay a hefty compensation, not that money can atone for Alexis's actions. Plus, her family will have to be informed of her *random assault*. She'll say someone got rough on her while she was working the streets. That's what they all say, but the prostitutes talk among themselves. Hopefully, they'll stay far away from my brother in the future.

"I'll get her name to you," I say. "Send me the bill." Of course, it'll include a big fat bonus for the doctor.

Without wasting more time, I get my car and drive to my parents' house. On the way, I call my father and tell him I'll be there shortly. It's almost three in the morning, but he doesn't share a bedroom with Maman, so I don't risk waking her up.

My father replies with, "I'll wait downstairs."

He knows I won't call at this hour unless there's a problem, usually one that involves a traitor or an unauthorized killing.

I kill the headlights before I pull through the gates. Maman's window faces the front lawn. Father stands in the dark by the door, flanked by two guards.

"Come in." He walks ahead of me to his study and only flicks the lights on when the door is closed. He's dressed in his silk robe and a pair of slippers. He pours two glasses of whiskey before taking the chair behind his desk. "What happened?"

I take out my phone and show him the picture I took of the woman in the hospital.

He lifts his gaze to me. "Alexis?"

My voice is clipped. "Yes."

Sighing, he rubs a hand over his face. "Is she going to make it?"

"I'm waiting for the doctor to text me, but I think so. She's not much worse than the previous one, and that one survived." I move closer. "However, the next one may not be so lucky."

"Fuck." My father slams a palm on the desk.

He understands the implications of murder. Taking out your

enemies is one thing. Taking out the very prostitutes you're pimping is quite another.

"We have to deal with Alexis," I say.

My father looks at me, his bad eye drooping more than usual. He doesn't want to punish his favorite son, but he knows he's let it go too far. If Alexis doesn't end up in jail soon, he'll end up with a bullet in the back of his head. These women have families. They're locals. Their fear of our power is only going to last so long before someone vengeful gets trigger happy. Besides, this is not the example we want to set.

"Fine," he says, pushing his chair away from the desk and getting to his feet. "Deal with him."

He can fucking count on that.

I leave his study with long steps. In the car, I dial Gautier. "Is Zoe home?"

"Yes, sir."

"Meet me at Alexis's and bring Benoit. Keep it discreet."

BACK AT ALEXIS'S PLACE, I find him a lot more sober than I left him. He's frightened, as he should be. He knows he fucked up one time too many. The fucker who was with him is still there. Good. At least the man was intelligent enough to do as I've instructed, to stay put. He knows better than to let me hunt him, because then he would've been a free kill.

Alexis is pacing the floor, a bag of peas pressed to his swollen eye. "What the fuck took you so long? Where have you been?"

"Home."

He stops. The color drains from his face. "Home?"

Crossing my arms, I enjoy his palpable fear. "To see father."

He swallows. "Max, listen, I—"

I turn to his buddy, one of the men I've seen frequently at the port. "What's your name?"

The man is so rigid it looks like his spine may snap. "Francois Leclerc, sir."

Alexis may be my father's son, but I'm the fucking underboss, and they both know I come with my father's blessing. Right now that makes me the boss.

"Who's the woman?"

Alexis points at a handbag that lies on the table. I go over and pick it up. It's imitation leather, a cheap quality. The plastic is cracked. Unzipping it, I take out a wallet. There's an ID card inside. I pocket it and take the bag, then tilt my head toward the door. "Let's go."

Alexis drops the bag of peas. "Where?"

I smile. "For a ride."

Francois turns as white as baguette pastry.

"Bring your toy," I say to him.

He frowns, looking at me with a retarded expression.

"Your whip," I say. "Go fetch it."

He starts to tremble. "It's not mine." He points at Alexis. "It's his."

"Did I fucking ask you whose it is?"

"No, sir."

"Then move your ass."

Looking at me from over his shoulder as if he expects me to shoot him in the back, he scurries down the hallway and returns with the whip.

"After you." Stepping aside, I wait for them to pass in front of me.

They don't argue. Arguing will only make what's waiting for them worse. Alexis grins as he passes, but it's all acting. The coward is shaking in his pants.

Benoit and Gautier have arrived. They're waiting downstairs. Benoit drives Francois while Gautier and I take Alexis with us. We don't speak. It's only when we near the warehouse at the docks where we torture our rivals that Alexis start to shift in the backseat.

"You're going to shoot me?" he asks snidely. "Your own brother?"

I don't bother to grace him with a reply.

After we've parked, Gautier escorts the two men to the warehouse. I take my Glock from the cubbyhole and slip it into my waistband before taking the whip. Benoit unlocks the warehouse door and flicks the light on.

"Wait by the car," I tell Gautier. I hand the woman's ID card and handbag to Benoit. "Get this to Dr. Olivier."

They nod and leave.

Alexis and Francois stand in a pool of light that falls from a single naked bulb when I enter the warehouse.

"Strip," I say. It's the same order I've given Zoe only a few hours ago and for the very same reason—to punish and teach a lesson.

The men don't move.

I take out the gun. "I can motivate you with a bullet in your foot." I step closer. "Maybe one in the hand, too."

At that, Francois starts unbuttoning his shirt. My reputation is solid. I'm a man of my word. No idle threats. I've worked hard on establishing that honor. That's why I let no one off the hook, not even my flower.

Alexis follows suit, hatred burning in his swollen eyes. His nose is askew. I've broken it. Good. I love the bruises blooming on his jaw.

I circle them like a shark, gun clutched in my hand, until they stand naked. Their cocks are flaccid.

Tapping the barrel of the gun against Francois's temple, I say. "Get him hard."

He turns his head quickly to look at me, slobber flying from his mouth. "What?"

I point at Alexis's soft dick. "Get it up."

Alexis growls. "What the fuck?"

"Shut up." I press the gun barrel on Alexis's hand, right above his trigger finger. "Do you need motivation?"

He's seen me torture our enemies before. He knows what I'm capable of. Gritting his teeth, he shakes his head.

Francois faces my brother reluctantly. Sweat beads on his forehead as he grips my brother's cock in his fist. Pinching his eyes shut, he turns his head away and starts pumping. The sick pervert that my brother is, he gets hard.

I kick a bench toward Francois. "Bend over."

He stumbles a step back. "What?"

"You heard me."

Walking with slow steps to the bench, he bends over, leaning his shaking arms on the wood. He looks at me from over his shoulder, his chin wobbling.

I give Alexis a shove. "Fuck him."

Alexis rounds on me, his eyes huge. "What?"

"Shove your dick in his ass and fuck him like you mean it, or you both get a bullet in the hand. I can guarantee you'll never use a gun again."

Alexis curses, but he goes forward. Inwardly, I smile. My brother isn't only a coward, he's also the worst kind, the kind who'd turn on a friend to save his own skin. He'd rather fuck his buddy in the ass than be the one who's fucked, which is why I'm letting him have a go first. I can't wait to see his face when it's his turn. They're going to fuck each other until their dicks are limp and then again. I'm going to whip them to shreds while they do it.

Picking up the whip, I tighten my fingers around the handle. I've been looking forward to this for a long time, and I have all night.

CHAPTER 25

Zoe

It's dawn, and Maxime is still not home. I've been pacing up and down, unable to think about anything but that woman, unable to get the images out of my head. I'm still dressed in the red ballroom gown and Maxime's jacket, my ass smarting from his belt, yet I feel extremely lucky, lucky that I'm not that girl. Knowing how easily that could've been me makes me sick. It leaves me with unanswered questions about who this family is and why they took me. If only I had access to the internet, I could've done my own research. I wish I could've called Maxime, but my phone is in the clutch bag we left at the hotel.

When I can't stand on my feet any longer, I go to the foyer and sit on the bottom of the stairs. I don't know how much time passes, if it's minutes or hours, but when the front door finally opens, I jump up and rush forward. Maxime stands on the step, my coat and clutch in one hand. For a second, we just look at each other. His hair is messy and his jaw dark with stubble. His coat hangs open. Splatters of blood decorate his white shirt. He's lost the bowtie, the top two buttons of his shirt undone.

"How is she?" I ask breathlessly.

"Fine." He strides past me into the house, leaving the door open.

A gust of cold wind follows him inside. I shut the door and just stand there, feeling useless, left in the dark.

"Maxime."

He stops, but he doesn't turn to look at me.

"What did the doctor say?" I ask.

"She'll be discharged by tomorrow. Stop worrying your pretty little head over her."

Stop worrying? I go after him, catching up just as he reaches the stairs. Moving around him, I climb two stairs to put us on eye level. "Do you hear yourself? Are you insane?"

The corner of his mouth pulls up. "We've established that already. Move aside, Zoe. I need a shower."

"Do you even give a damn?" I cry out.

"Yes." His jaw bunches. "Which is why Alexis and his friend have been punished."

"Is that where you've been all night?"

He looks me over. "You should've changed and gone to bed."

"There's no way I could've just put my head down and gone to sleep without knowing if she's all right."

"I told you." He lifts a brow. "Anything else you need to know?"

I consider my question and the impact it will have on an already fragile situation, but I can't go another day without the truth. "Why did you take me? What do you want from Damian?"

He watches me steadily, his gray eyes flat, but there's something underneath the coldness, something he's hiding.

"Tell me, Maxime. I deserve the truth." It's the least he can give me for stealing my life.

He mounts one step, two, putting our bodies flush. "Have you learned nothing, tonight?"

"That I'm supposed to trust you blindly?" I bite out, craning my neck to look up at him.

He grips the tangled mess of hair at the back of my head, but it's not an angry move. It's tender. "There are things I can't tell you. I can't always explain my actions. If you don't give me reason to do otherwise, I will always act in your best interest." His steely gaze pierces mine. "That's why you have to trust me. Always. No matter what."

I blink up at him, letting the information sink in, pondering a different question that has been haunting me all night. "Why didn't you give me to Alexis?"

He releases me. "We've been through this."

He's not giving me anything, nothing to piece the puzzle together, only the bit about trusting him without question. My life is spiraling out of control, and I feel lost. I don't have the facts to gather my ammunition and shield myself from the mind games he's playing. I'm at a disadvantage in our war, and I'm afraid I'm losing my grip.

Reading my expression correctly, he asks, "What are you so scared of, Zoe?"

I give him the truth. "I don't even know who I am anymore."

He trails his gaze over me, taking me in from my bare feet to my clean-scrubbed face. His words are soft-spoken, a complete contrast to earlier tonight. "When I look at you, I don't see a whore."

Tears spring to my eyes. No matter how he looks at me, I can never wipe those stains on my soul away. I am what he made me, and suddenly the truth I've been avoiding all night hits me squarely in the chest. I want to believe him. Badly. I want to believe that I'm somehow something more, but it's just my psyche's way of trying to protect itself.

Cupping my cheek, he draws a thumb over my jaw. "How you look at yourself is entirely up to you." Then he moves me aside and climbs past me up the stairs.

I'm drowning in helplessness, torn between wanting to grab the lie he offers between both hands and clinging to the last shreds of truth in my soul. I'm weak, so damn weak, because I don't want to end up like that woman—fuck, I don't even know her name, like she's no one—and I hate myself for it.

"Maxime."

He stops again.

"Please let me go outside," I say. "I need some air."

He hesitates.

"I'm not going anywhere." My hand trembles on the balustrade. "You've made that clear."

Keeping his back turned to me, he nods once before continuing his ascend.

When the bedroom door slams upstairs, I go through the kitchen to the backdoor. A guard stands aside when I exit. He seems surprised, but he doesn't stop me. I walk barefoot over the gravel to the maze, but I don't want to lose myself in more puzzles. Instead, I take the path to the cliffs and follow it to the spot from where Maxime had jumped. The pebbles and sticks are sharp under my feet. I welcome the pain. Even after last night, I still need the punishment. I'm freezing. The wind is cold and relentless, blowing the edges of Maxime's jacket open and exposing my naked shoulders. I embrace the bite, hoping it will freeze everything inside me, but the burning in my gut continues, eating me up like a ravenous monster. My pain shines like precious stones in the dusty bed of a river. My feelings are discarded like diamonds in the dust. Wasted.

I STARE out over the sea. It's breathtakingly beautiful. The sun is kissing the horizon. It gives the cold blue of the ocean a golden glow. Even in the stark gray of dusk, the water in the cove below is turquoise. A white beach hugs it, just like the one where we had the picnic. Sharp rocks are scattered treacherously throughout the bay, I'm guessing making it difficult for boats to anchor here. It's like a small slice of paradise in hell.

Slowly, I edge forward, until my toes hang over the cliff. My body screams at me to go back to safer ground as fear claws its way through my chest. It's a fear I'm no longer unfamiliar with, the fear for my life. Self-preservation kicks in, making me tremble and sweat, making me feel sick when I peer down. I'm a coward. I could've fought Maxime harder. I surrendered too easily. I hate myself. I hate feeling helpless and weak. I take another pace until only my heels are resting on the rocks, my stomach climbing up in my throat as my body sways in the strong wind.

"Zoe."

I turn my head at the sound of my name. It's instinctive. It's a trained reaction, like a dog minding a whistle. Maxime stands on the path, a distance away from me. He's wearing nothing but a pair of tracksuit pants. His chest and feet are bare, his scars exposed to the elements.

He raises an arm. "Give me your hand, little flower."

I look back down at the sea, scary but oh so pretty. I'm tired of being weak. I want to jump like him. I want to jump and know I can survive. Carefully, I lift my right foot, posing it over the abyss.

"Zoe! Look at me."

The last I hear is Maxime's howl as I face my demons and step over the edge.

~ TO BE CONTINUED ~

ALSO BY CHARMAINE PAULS

DIAMOND MAGNATE NOVELS

(Dark Romance)

Standalone Novel

(Dark Forced Marriage Romance)

Beauty in the Broken

Diamonds are Forever Trilogy

(Dark Mafia Romance)

Diamonds in the Dust

Diamonds in the Rough

Diamonds are Forever

Box Set

Beauty in the Stolen Trilogy

(Dark Romance)

Stolen Lust

Stolen Life

Stolen Love

Box Set

The White Nights Duet

(Contemporary Romance)

White Nights

Midnight Days

The Loan Shark Duet

(Dark Mafia Romance)

Dubious

Consent

Box Set

The Age Between Us Duet

(Older Woman Younger Man Romance)

Old Enough

Young Enough

Box Set

Standalone Novels

(Enemies-to-Lovers Dark Romance)

Darker Than Love

(Second Chance Romance)

Catch Me Twice

Krinar World Novels

(Futuristic Romance)

The Krinar Experiment

The Krinar's Informant

7 Forbidden Arts Series

(Fated Mates Paranormal Romance)

Pyromancist (Fire)

Aeromancist, The Beginning (Prequel)

Aeromancist (Air)

Hydromancist (Water)

Geomancist (Earth)

Necromancist (Spirit)

ABOUT THE AUTHOR

Charmaine Pauls was born in Bloemfontein, South Africa. She obtained a degree in Communication at the University of Potchefstroom and followed a diverse career path in journalism, public relations, advertising, communication, and brand marketing. Her writing has always been an integral part of her professions.

When she moved to Chile with her French husband, she started writing full-time. She has been publishing novels and short stories since 2011. Charmaine currently lives in Montpellier, France with her family. Their household is a lively mix of Afrikaans, English, French, and Spanish.

Join Charmaine's mailing list
https://charmainepauls.com/subscribe/

Join Charmaine's readers' group on Facebook
http://bit.ly/CPaulsFBGroup

Read more about Charmaine's novels and short stories on
https://charmainepauls.com

Connect with Charmaine

Facebook
http://bit.ly/Charmaine-Pauls-Facebook

Amazon
http://bit.ly/Charmaine-Pauls-Amazon

Goodreads
http://bit.ly/Charmaine-Pauls-Goodreads

Twitter
https://twitter.com/CharmainePauls

Instagram
https://instagram.com/charmainepaulsbooks

BookBub
http://bit.ly/CPaulsBB

TikTok
https://www.tiktok.com/@charmainepauls

Made in the USA
Columbia, SC
23 February 2022